I0723135

Light Up My Heart

A POINT PERRY CHRISTMAS

HEARTS OF POINT PERRY

JOANNE SPEIRS

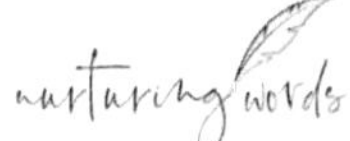

Ebook ISBN: 978-1-76357-900-2

Print ISBN: 9798332538919

Editors: Sandy Vaile, Lauren McKellar

Proofreader: Madeline Ash

Cover: Louisa West

This book is dedicated to
The Wednesday Wonder Women
Heather and Lou
You are my queens 🩶

And to Rachelle
I appreciate you 🩶

Author's Note

Hello readers,

Light Up My Heart: A Point Perry Christmas is feel-good, small-town, opposites attract romance written in Australian English. So, depending on where you're reading my book, you might find a 's' instead of 'z' or some other spelling variation. There is also use of Australian slang such as 'ambo' for ambulance and Aussie-specific words like 'road train' for long trucks and 'petrol bowser' which are gas pumps in America.

Thanks for reading Ryan and Scarlett's story and I hope you fall in love with Point Perry.

Trigger warning: panic attack (on page), near drowning (on page), workplace bullying (off page), rejected by parents, abuse, abandonment (off page).

Jo

CHAPTER 1

Scarlett

The foul, dusty north wind gusts through the door, held open by a customer who seems stuck with their eyes fixed on the road train rumbling back onto the highway. Grit and sand swirl at their feet and across the service station shop floor, which I've swept five times already today. This is what you get when living in a small town surrounded by sandy beaches, wild ocean and dry paddocks. I'm on the verge of losing my patience and yelling at them to quit dawdling when I remember working here is temporary, so I take a deep breath and release it with a sigh.

Besides, I only need to keep up the façade of having returned home for a holiday for a week ... until Christmas is over and I can run back to the tatters of my life in Adelaide city.

Who on God's earth would be out in this weather, I have no idea. With it being the weekend before Christmas, Point Perry has been abuzz with last-minute shoppers, family visits and gearing up for the Lighting of the Jetty.

But today, everyone seems to have bunkered down in air-conditioned holiday houses, caravans or shacks. Even the petrol bowsers I've been manning for my older brother Curly have been quiet, which is a blessing, as it's given me time to update my resume, draft a cover letter and reply to some emails about my previous employer in between stacking cans of soft drinks into the service station's fridges. The things I do to help my brother's business when he's down a staff member and he has children to mind.

Curly has a way of guilt shaming—it's been five years since I've come back to Point Perry, and this is the first Christmas we'll all be together on the farm. My parents are under the impression that all is well with me and I'll return to Adelaide and my job before the new year, and given the amount of work and stress they have with the farm, I don't want to be the cause of additional worry and disappointment for them. And I'm a thirty-two-year-old grown woman who should be able to keep her shit together. Alas, it seems not.

So, I'm here for a week under a cloud of lies while looking for a new job to pay my mortgage, my credit card and my car loan. No biggy.

But nothing, not being unemployed or even this sweltering, revolting weather, will sour my Christmas cheer. Choosing not to scold the dawdling door person, I opt for a more festive approach by singing the chorus of 'We Wish You a Merry Christmas', complete with finger clicking, and enjoy the refreshing gust of cool air from the open fridge door.

I finish with some drum beats on an empty box before standing with a little spring and coming face-to-face with a wall of blue. Blue legs that go up and up ... and up. A Point Perry District Hospital logo sits next to the V neckline of his scrubs shirt, exposing lovely and tanned skin with a sprinkling of hair. I swallow. This guy is ... large. He's as solidly built as Curly, with a physique that could rival a brick outhouse. My head perfectly aligns with his shoulder. Sandalwood and sea salt tickle my nose. My eyes briefly flutter closed, and when my head involuntarily tilts back and I open my eyes, I'm met with a … scowl.

I jerk back. The scruffy jawline, messy dark hair that stands on end, most likely from the gale outside, and the rugged appearance all contribute to his rough and untamed look. But it's his eyes that take my breath away. Not because they're dazzling and bright and sexy but because they're … sad. Blue eyes that are so incredibly, utterly sad. How could anybody be so morose at such a joyous time?

'Excuse me.' Scowl Man reaches past and grabs a bottle of water from the fridge, brushing past my shoulder when he retreats.

His voice gives me goosebumps, or that could be the air con kicking back in now that the shop door is closed. Or could it be that I just can't stand jerks?

'You're most welcome.' The words come out through gritted teeth and a fake smile. I step back, and my foot catches the edge of something … that moves. A black wheel flips around and, as I nearly take a tumble, it goes scooting across the shop floor.

'Oh dear, be careful, love,' a recognisable voice says. 'Sorry. I shouldn't have parked my walker right behind you.' A well-weathered and ring-laden hand circles my upper arm. As I turn, I'm met with the familiar sight of dear old Aunt Lilac, who must've snuck in when the door was open. Her hair, dyed in a purple rinse, perfectly complements the various shades of purple she wears from head to toe.

Scowl Man steps around me, latches onto Aunt Lilac's elbow with one hand, and drapes his other arm around her shoulder. 'I've got you, young lady. Here, let's get you back on your walker and we'll pop the brakes on this time, shall we?'

Aunt Lilac flutters her eyelashes and gives him a blinding smile. 'You sure do know how to make an oldie like me feel all gooey inside.'

'Only for you, Lilac, and what are you doing out on a day like this? Didn't you hear the hot weather health warning? With the temp getting to forty-two degrees, the best place for you is at home, not out and about.'

Once Aunt Lilac settles on the walker seat, I hand her an open bottle of water. Without hesitation, she takes a generous swig.

'I was actually coming to see this one.' Her bony finger points to me. My eyebrows shoot up to the bottom of the Santa hat perched on my head.

'Whatever you're going to rope me into, Aunt Lilac, I can't do it. I'm only here until Boxing Day, and my dear brother has me working and babysitting my niece and nephew while Justine gets things ready for the Lighting of the Jetty and our Christmas Day festivities out at the farm.'

Like the star atop a Christmas tree, her eyes shine with a brilliant twinkle. 'That is perfect. I only need you until Christmas Eve.'

I purse my lips. Aunt Lilac has her finger in many pies—the CWA, lawn bowls, local theatre group ... 'Go on.'

'I need a lead singer for the town choir because the motley crew I have are ... well ... let's just say, you will make it *a lot* better.'

That was not what I was expecting. My tummy flips in anticipation. It seems all my Christmases have come at once.

'I'd be honoured, Aunt Lilac. I love singing, and I love Christmas.'

CHAPTER 2

Ryan

I can't even buy bread and milk from the servo without Christmas cheer being shoved down my throat. Who sings a Christmas carol when they greet their customers … in a voice that sounds like an angel? Scarlett Reynolds, that's who. There's no mistaking her long, straight, dark chocolate hair and curious hazel eyes. And those freckles scattered across her cheeks that I would recognise anywhere. I'd heard she was back in Point Perry for Christmas but had no idea she had the voice to rival Taylor Swift.

No wonder Lilac wants her in the town choir.

Scarlett's face lights up in a grin as big as if she'd won Powerball. She holds the door open while Lilac shuffles out. The fluffy ball on the tip of her Santa hat flaps in the wind. Our eyes lock for the briefest moment. There's no flicker of recognition, though, which sends a stab of annoyance through me, but I don't blame her; it has been fifteen years since *that* summer.

'Let me give you a lift home, Lilac. I don't want to be fixing you up for heat stroke at the hospital later.' I follow Lilac through the servo door and outside, heading to my station wagon, where I hold the front door open for her. Scarlett trails behind and lingers in the shade.

'Don't you need to get what you came for?' Lilac asks.

'I was craving some of Conway's butterscotch ice cream and need bread and milk, but I can come back later.'

'Okay, then. Thank you for the lift. I am feeling a bit hot and bothered, but I had to catch Scarlett before she headed back out to the farm.'

Before I can reach her, her eyes roll back in her head, and her body begins to sway unsteadily. I lunge. It all happens in slow motion. Scarlett and I surge towards her. Neither of us make it. With a wobbly step, Lilac tries to sit on her walker but loses her balance, stumbling and tumbling off. Her arm reaches out to break her fall; she lands on her side, knocking her head on the concrete next to the petrol bowser.

'Aunt Lilac.' Scarlett is by her side, one hand on the older woman's leg, the other on her forehead.

I crouch on the other side. It's second nature to scan her body and assess the surroundings. 'Don't move her. She landed heavily on her arm and banged her head. Can you call the ambulance?'

Scarlett's eyes find mine as she pulls a mobile phone from the back pocket of her denim shorts. They are wide with worry, but she does as I ask, conveying my assessments to the operator. The gold glitter adorning her eyelids sparkles, and her Christmas tree earrings flip around as another gust of dusty, sandy wind picks up an empty chip packet and blows it past the bowser.

Of all the days and all the places for Lilac to have a fall … Sweat pools at the base of my spine and trickles from my temple down my cheek. The wind feels like someone blowing a hair dryer on my face. My mouth is parched. Thank God it's late enough in the day for there to be shade and the cement, although warm, hasn't been in the sun, so it won't burn Lilac's skin.

As Scarlett finishes the call, Lilac groans and tries to lift her head.

'Lilac, you've had a fall. Just stay still while I check a few things, okay?' I run my hand down Lilac's spine from the base of her skull and across her hips. Everything feels in order, and Lilac doesn't respond to any pain. 'Where do you hurt?'

'It's my bloody arm.' Lilac winces and groans, then attempts to roll over onto her back.

'Just stay where you are, Lilac. Don't try to move. I think you might've broken something. That's probably why it hurts.' I hope to God it's nothing more than her wrist, and a simple break at that—otherwise, she'll be off to Adelaide for surgery, which is not ideal at any time, but especially at this time of year.

'My head hurts too.' She tries to lift her head, but it lolls to the side.

'Are you on any medication, Lilac?' I press my fingers to her other wrist. Her pulse is racing. Adrenaline. Something I'm all too familiar with.

'You work at the hospital. Don't you know?'

'Yes, I work at the hospital, but Doctor Cruickshank is the only person who knows your medication.'

'Ah, just my blood pressure tablets.' Another groan reverberates through her body.

'Scarlett, can you grab a wet towel, a solid cardboard box and the first aid kit? Here.' I pull my mobile phone from the back pocket of my scrubs, Face ID it and hand it over to Scarlett. 'Can you call Barb Rogers? You know Barb, right?' She nods, and the bell on her hat tinkles. 'Her number is under "boss". Let her know what's happened and to be on standby.'

While she's gone, I continue my assessment of Lilac,

asking her questions to determine if she has a concussion—she passes with flying colours.

Confident it's only a broken wrist and a head knock, I carefully roll her onto her back. As the pressure is lifted off her arm, Lilac lets out an almighty scream. 'You're okay, Lilac. Try and take a few deep breaths for me.'

As much as it pains me, I need to keep her awake and talking, keep her mind off the pain until the ambos arrive. So, I ask the only question I know will achieve that. 'Tell me about the Christmas choir, Lilac. What songs have you got planned?'

As Lilac lists the carols and places they'll be singing, Scarlett returns, hands loaded with a pile of sodden face washers, the first aid kit and a flattened Coke box under her arm. She rests a towel on Lilac's forehead and uses another to dab at her cheeks.

Using pieces of the box and a bandage from the first aid kit, Scarlett helps with the makeshift splint, supporting Lilac's wrist before gently resting it on her stomach.

'Lilac'—I gently cradle her hand in mine—'I need to take all these rings off your fingers as your hand will swell and it's most likely you'll need a plaster. Is that okay?'

'Give them to Scarlett, please.'

'Now, you'll probably be in hospital for a day or two, so I'll drop your walker back home; you won't be able to use it for a while.'

Lilac lets out a frustrated sigh and winces. 'Okay, then. Bloody hell.'

With five golden rings removed, and after making her as comfortable as possible, thankfully, it's only another couple of minutes before the St John's Ambulance arrives—the bumper of their rig and windscreen wipers covered in gold tinsel. Seems I can't escape the festive season. I let out a sigh and hand Lilac over to Deb and Bronte—the volunteer paramedics —who load her into the ambulance.

'Scarlett, dear, Ryan said I'll be out of action for a few days, so you're in charge of the choir now. Come and see me at the hospital so I can fill you in. You have a busy schedule and a lot of Christmas cheer to share.'

'Oh, Aunt Lilac, okay. I'll pop in tomorrow.' Scarlett leans in and squeezes her good hand. 'You take care, okay?'

'I'm in good hands with the handsome Nurse Ryan.' As Lilac sucks on the green whistle, a mischievous glint dances in her eyes, followed by a knowing smile.

'I'll see you there, Lilac.' I close the ambulance door and tap it a couple of times so Deb knows she can head to the hospital.

As the ambulance turns onto the main road into Point Perry, Scarlett steps up next to me. 'Poor dear. Hope she'll be up and about for the jetty lighting. It's such a great night. Will you be going?' She turns to me, her face full of excitement like she's a kid in a candy store. 'Oh, and I'm Scarlett. Curly's younger sister.'

Her hand is ready for me to shake. I debate whether to take it, still pissed she doesn't recognise me. Despite my initial hesitation, I eventually relent. 'I'm someone from your past, fifteen years to be exact, and I hate Christmas with a passion.'

CHAPTER 3

Scarlett

'Oh, love, what are you doing up there on top of the ladder?' Mum's voice is full of concern as she leans against the shed door. 'You're not looking for more Christmas decorations, are you? The house and yard already look like Santa's workshop.'

Sliding a cardboard box across the metal shelf, I can't help but chuckle, but in the process, I inadvertently score a mouthful of dirt. 'I know you secretly love it, Mum.'

'I do, but ... your father will be back soon; let him get up there.'

'Mum, it will be safer for me to do it.' A trail of dried mice droppings sits between the next boxes. A shiver snakes across my shoulders at the memory of the mouse plague and the time when the rodents were in my bedroom. 'Do you know where my glory box is?'

'Would that be this one on the end of the shelf that says "glory box"?' Mum lifts onto her tiptoes and taps the edge of the box.

'Smarty pants.' I carefully descend the ladder and move it along.

'Dare I ask why?' Mum shuffles over and holds the sides of the ladder as I step up.

'I'm trying to solve a mystery.' About a guy who said the strangest thing before hightailing to his car and racing off after the ambulance, leaving me no chance to ask him what the heck he was on about. 'And sorry about my bum in your face.'

'And what a nice bum it is.' She gives it a cheeky pinch.

I miss this fun banter we have. The infrequent FaceTime calls aren't the same. 'In fact, you would know. Who is the male nurse at the hospital?'

'Oh, um, he's not been here long. Just a few months, and I've not had the pleasure of meeting him, but Marge and Greta in the café said he's very good-looking and a lovely man.'

I steal a quick glance down at Mum. There's something in her voice ... 'Are you blushing? I can't believe the three of you. Do you know his name by chance?'

'Ooh, let me think. Raymond or Robert. Starts with an R.'

'Well, you're no help at all. Maybe next time you can jot this type of important information down so you don't forget.'

'Yes, ma'am.' Mum lets out a light-hearted laugh. 'I'll throw a notepad and pen into my handbag and take them wherever I go.'

'Please do!'

While I'm grinning at Mum's retort, my brain flicks through all the people I knew with names starting with R and come up blank. I set the box on the concrete floor, shoving a rusted tin of nails to the side to make room. After folding a dirty hessian sack in half, I place it on the floor and kneel. When I pull off the box's lid and give it a shake, a cloud of dust and a few dead flies and millipedes scatter onto the floor.

The sudden rush of memories takes me by surprise, hitting me in the chest with a bittersweet intensity.

Sitting on top is a patchwork quilt of faded yellows,

creams and florals, made gaudy by the mission brown spacer squares. A couple of moth balls fall to the floor as I gently unfold it. The whirr of the sewing machines in the school home economics room plays in my mind. The teacher's name ... no idea. Why did I keep this quilt? Also, no idea.

'Oh, I remember that.' Mum peers over my shoulder. 'Actually, I remember the hissy fit you threw when the haberdashery shop didn't have the "rust" colour you wanted, and you had to settle for "poo" brown.'

A little laugh slips out. 'Trust you to remember that and not the nurse's name.'

However, the mission brown sparks a nostalgic memory. Of warm summer days, a boy, a kissing session in the back of Dad's old Sandman (What happened to that car?), that nearly led to something else. Then didn't. Then he went home to the city like all the holidaymakers did every summer.

Under the quilt is my Point Perry Area School year twelve jacket. Red with the black school emblem—wheat and fish—and all our names printed on the back. All fourteen names. The name I'm looking for doesn't jump out, but a gazillion other things do. Ah, the good ol' school days.

I remove three Barbie dolls (and their associated outfits and furniture), a pair of sheep shears, a hand fishing reel still with a squid jig attached but the barbs rusted, and a tissue box cover I lovingly crafted with floral fabric, pink ribbon and copious amounts of craft glue.

There are six *Sweet Valley High* books and two diaries (locked and with no key), and last—and what I'm looking for —is a bundle of letters. The faint smell of Impulse body spray is so familiar when I press the letters to my nose.

'Aha. Found them.'

'Found what, love?' Mum returns from the shelves, a knot of fairy lights in her hand and a deep frown on her face.

'These.' I hold up a wad of browned envelopes tied

together with a white ribbon that's stamped with red love hearts. 'I have a hunch the good nurse's name is in these.'

Mum looks at me like I've grown another head.

'He said he knew me from fifteen years ago. That's the year I finished school, and that Christmas holiday, I remember we had a lot of bonfires on the beach by the caravan park. I had my Ps and was driving the Sandman.'

'Scarlett, dear, your cheeks have turned the same colour as your name.'

I press the back of my hand to my cheek, and yes, it's warm. It's stifling in the shed. Mum's eyebrows raise.

My mouth is suddenly as dry as the northerly. 'Well, it's a bit embarrassing telling you what I got up to those summers when I was a teen.'

'You think I don't know?' She's grinning like the cat that caught the mouse. 'Word always got back to me, and us mums were keeping tabs on you. Small town and all.'

'Muuummm. And all this time I thought you had no idea.' Because my knees are killing me, I scoot back and settle on my bum. The somewhat cool of the concrete is a relief in the stuffy shed.

Mum pulls over an old drink bottle crate, turns it upside down and sits. 'Hurry up and just yank the ribbon, will you.' Mum does a 'chop-chop' motion with her hands. 'We have a mystery to solve.'

Doing as I'm told—which I'm never very good at, and it's why I'm back home after five years—I untie the ribbon, open the top envelope, pull the letter out and ... 'Ryan Black'.

The boy I thought I fell in love with during the summer of 2008.

CHAPTER 4

Ryan

Scarlett's standing in the doorway of the staff lunchroom, hands on hips, that stupid Santa hat still perched on her head. She's changed into a different pair of short shorts—making her already long legs look longer —and a white tee with a Christmas tree-shaped quote that reads: I'm too hot for ugly Christmas jumpers.

'Bloody hell,' I mutter under my breath.

'Why didn't you just tell me who you were ... Ryan Black?' she demands. 'And why are you moving the Christmas tree behind the door where no one will see it?'

There's a stirring in my gut, and it's not because I missed lunch. I'm so close to her that I can see the sprinkle of freckles kissing her nose and cheeks. They don't seem to have faded over the years. Her nose squishes like it used to, and a frown wrinkles her forehead when I don't answer. It's her 'impatient' look.

'Well?' Her head tips to the side, and her eyes widen, perhaps to emphasise the question.

Yes, it's been over a decade, but our brief time together seemed to have left little impression on her, considering she didn't recognise me immediately. Sure, we had a fun couple of weeks of summer together and did all the things frisky teenagers do. Well, except for one thing. We were sensible, and I admired her for knowing what she wanted and didn't want. She's the first girl I had ever crushed on, and I've never forgotten her or how she made me feel. She gave me hope— gave me a glimpse of something better. But then—

'Like I told you earlier, I hate Christmas, and this tree is just plain annoying and in your face. I don't want to spend the few breaks I get looking at the hideous thing when I have to endure all the other "stuff" everywhere else.' I leave the question about my identity unanswered as I'm loving the way she's biting her bottom lip and then clenching her jaw. It's at total odds with her festive outfit that screams *over the top*. And it's sexy as hell. I could be in deep trouble here. There was no way of knowing Scarlett would be coming home when I accepted the placement in Point Perry a couple of months ago. I'm considering whether I should request a few more days of annual leave and escape town during this silly season. I make a mental note to check the roster.

'And the Ryan Black thing?' Her eyebrows shoot up with expectation.

I release a sigh. 'I was curious to see if you remembered me. But obviously, that summer was forgettable, and I was just another guy to add to your holiday flings. You probably had heaps of them growing up here.' Shit, that's a bit of a low blow, and I probably shouldn't have said it, but it seems there's some unresolved resentment happening.

'I can't believe you just said that. But I'm glad you brought it up. Yes, I'll admit I didn't recognise you *straight away*, but you were familiar, just older and ... different. You didn't have a three-day growth when you were seventeen. And I don't remember what most of the kids in my class looked like and I saw them all day, every day since kindy, so how am I supposed to remember you?' It's her turn to let out a frustrated sigh. 'And while we're talking about remembering, you obviously forgot me quick smart too. I bet you went right on home to the big city and got another chick.'

That, I was not expecting. Why would she think that? I wrote to her for about six months before I gave up. My turn to frown. She frowns back. It's like a frowning competition. I clench my jaw; she does the same. Neither of us speaks.

'You're unbelievable.' Scarlett breaks the stand-off. Hands fly from her hips to the white fluffy ball dangling from the end of the hat. She squeezes it. A rendition of 'Jingle Bells' plays, but the music is muted, a little slurred, as if perhaps her hat is running out of batteries. With determined eyes, she says, 'I'll see you around. Or not ... Ryan Black. And tell Lilac I'll be back in the morning.' And she turns and power walks towards the hospital entrance, all sass and determination. Stopping to look at her phone, she shakes her head and jams it into the pocket on the back of those short shorts.

What just happened in the space of three minutes? My grumpy arse sent her walking. I scrub a hand over my face, calling, 'Scarlett, wait.'

As I step through the door to go after her, the call button buzzer sounds above the nurses' station. It's Lilac. When I turn back to the front doors, they are closing behind Scarlett.

She doesn't give me a backward glance.

CHAPTER 5

Ryan

'Ryan, dear, I'm sorry to bother you when you must be busy.' Lilac uses the remote control for the bed to raise her head, adjusting her position so that she's sitting up.

If only she knew what she'd just interrupted. With her uninjured arm, Lilac fusses about in an oversized leather bag one of the locals must've dropped in. It hasn't taken long for word to get around about her accident and hospital stay. When I go to help, she slaps my hand away. 'I can do it. I'm not an invalid.'

I bite my tongue as she pulls out a manilla folder chock-full of papers. One slips out and flutters to the floor. When I reach down to pick it up, I notice it's sheet music for 'Away in a Manger'. I flinch like it's a poisonous snake about to strike.

'It's not going to hurt you, dear.' Lilac's tone is matter-of-fact.

In the short time I've been in Point Perry, I've come to realise she doesn't beat around the bush.

'In fact, it might do you good. If you plan on staying in

town for longer than the last few locums and nurses, like we all hope you do, being involved in the community is a way of life. You don't want to get on the wrong side of the locals now, do you? Tongues are probably already wagging about your anti-Christmas antics.'

Is Scarlett considered a local? I sure as hell have managed to get on her wrong side. Serves me right for being an arse. And I'm more than happy to be involved in the community, join the volunteer firefighters, play footy and cricket, and deliver meals to those who need them—I just want nothing to do with Christmas. I have my limits, and Christmas is a hard no.

Sheet music in hand, I meet Lilac's eyes. There's a glint in them, which is a good sign. My eyes flick to the monitors beside her bed—all good and stable. The bag of saline is nearly finished, and the colour's returned to her face. But a horrible bruise is spreading around her temple and eye. She's going to look a bit worse for wear for a while to come.

I hand the sheet back to her, but she doesn't take it, so I leave it on the bed. 'How's your pain?' I feel her fingers. 'Can you wiggle these for me?'

'Don't you go changing the subject with me, young man. I might be old, but I'm not blind.' She hands me another piece of paper from the folder. 'My pain is fine, and when can I go home?'

I check over her chart in the folder, skimming through her obs and notes. 'Well, I'm thinking Doctor Cruickshank will want you to stay for another day to keep an eye on that nasty bruise around your eye and to make sure you're comfortable with your arm. He'll be here for rounds later. He was called out for a home visit.'

'Oh, hope it wasn't anything serious. And don't be silly wasting his time. Now the shock's worn off, I feel fine.' She makes to swing a leg over the edge of the bed and promptly slumps back against the mattress. 'Just a bit dizzy.'

'Okay, Lilac, let's get you comfy again.' I slip my hand under her leg, lift it back on the mattress and pull up the blanket.

'I think I do need to stay put. Maybe just for tonight, anyway.' Her eyes flutter closed, and her shoulders slouch for a moment. It's like she's thinking, pondering what needs to be done. When they open again, that sparkle is back, and she slips a piece of paper into my hand. 'I have a job for you, then.'

When I unfold it, I'm greeted with a very shaky, hand-drawn mud map of Point Perry and some of the outer roads, which I've yet to discover. When did she have time to draw this? I only left her fifteen minutes ago.

On the map, she's circled the hardware store, the town hall (with a note saying choir practice) and the nursing home (with a note saying choir). The council office (with a note saying: Cr Giles) and jetty, with squiggles that resemble lights and a tree and little squares with 'market' written next to them. She's drawn a line indicating farther out of town, and at the end of a windy road, she's drawn a star with 'Reynolds' scribbled inside.

No, she is *not* sending me there. Lilac's eyebrows flicker up and down, teasing me. I can't—go there, that is. But a conceding sigh leaves my lips. 'Lilac, what's this map for?'

Although I already know, I have a ridiculous soft spot for Lilac, and I haven't been able to say no to her yet.

'Well, as you know, I'm the coordinator of the Christmas choir, and the Lighting of the Jetty and the Christmas markets are in a few days. Because I'm stuck in here, I can't coordinate things, but I need feet on the ground, so to speak ... oh, and two working arms.'

'And ...' I raise my eyebrows. 'You want me to ...?'

'For a good-looking nurse, you sure are daft. I might've

been a bit woozy at the petrol station, but I saw how you looked at young Scarlett. And then Greta—you know her from the café? Gossiping Greta? She brought my bag in—said Scarlett's only home for a week or so, and you've been looking a bit lonely, so maybe you could—what do the young ones say?—hook up.' She waggles her eyebrows. 'Give yourself a bit of festive cheer. Spend some time with her and have some fun. She might even show you around. There are lots of lovely places to visit you might not have had a chance to see yet.'

The scheming—'What exactly are you asking me to do?' I have no intention of spending any more time than necessary with Scarlett, especially not after her outburst just now. And especially not while she's all Christmassy cheer and jingle in my face. I'll be staying as far away as possible from that.

'Take this map and folder, follow this red line—which is a road if you haven't gathered—until you get to the star. It's the Reynolds' farm. That's where you'll find Scarlett. She needs this folder for the choir. Tell her to call me tomorrow or drop in, and I'll talk her through what needs to be done.'

My stubbornness kicks in and as much as I adore Lilac, she's pushing the boundaries. The last thing I need is another confrontation with the spritely Christmas elf and her singing hat. I look Lilac dead in the eyes. 'No can do. I'm rostered on late. And she told me she was coming in to see you tomorrow anyway. Which will be perfect. Then you can chat as much as you want for as long as you want.'

Lilac reaches over and presses the call button.

'Coming!' Barb bustles down the corridor, her shoes squeaking on the lino floor, and bursts into the room. 'Everything okay? You press the buzzer, Ryan?'

'No.' My answer comes out gruffer than intended. 'I mean, yes, everything is alright, and no, I didn't press the buzzer.'

'I did.' Lilac smirks. 'Barb, will it be okay if Ryan finishes up early tonight to run an errand for me? All in the name of community?'

Barb glances at her watch before her eyes meet Lilac's; she gives her a smile filled with understanding. 'I can't see why not unless we get an emergency. Tessa and Bev are here, too. Just make sure your phone is on. I'll call if needed.'

Lilac's smile is as sweet as pie. 'Well, perfect. Here.'

The folder is all but thrown at me. I cautiously raise my hands as if the paper is ablaze and instinctively step back. Nope, not happening. Lilac pokes me in the stomach with the end of the full-to-the-brim folder, and I retreat further. 'Lilac, she doesn't want to see me. We had a run-in just a while ago. The last thing she wants is for me to rock up on her doorstep.'

'But you only just met. What could you have possibly done in this short time to piss her off? Sorry about my cussing.'

'I'll leave you two to finish chatting.' Barb about turns and squeaks back to the reception desk.

'We …' I scratch the back of my head. Is Lilac as gossipy as Gossiping Greta? Is it worth the risk to get her off my case? Let's roll the dice and see. 'We have a past, Lilac. We know each other, but she didn't remember me today at the servo, and then she had a go at me for forgetting *her* and she stormed off. So, that's why I don't want to drive all the way out there and see her.'

'Well, young man, I may never have been married in my eighty-odd years, but I know a thing or two, and this'—she shakes the damn folder at me again—'is the answer. You need to sort it out, and this is the perfect way.'

I reluctantly step forward and snatch said folder.

'You can thank me later.' She winks.

I sigh, thank her, say my goodbyes and head down the corridor towards the break room to get my things out of my locker. When I swing open the break-room door, the damn

Christmas tree greets me—seems someone's moved it back to its prime position.

As I leave the hospital, 'The First Noel' plays overhead, and I grit my teeth.

I know it's unlikely, but I wonder if Scarlett's somehow responsible for this.

CHAPTER 6

Scarlett

Bless Mum for investing in a Thermomix. Our trip down memory lane this afternoon has included batches of rum balls, white Christmas, peppermint slice and mini Christmas puddings. The shiny white machine has crunched, whipped and mixed and, as per my usual baking style, there is not a clean patch on any benchtop. And I can't say just how many balls I've consumed.

My phone vibrates on the counter. *Gum Creek ELC* pops up on the screen. With a floury finger, I tap the decline button, as I've been doing all day, and I'll continue to do so until my former place of employment gets the message I no longer want anything to do with them.

'So, how is work going?' Mum flicks her eyes from the phone screen to the oven. She pulls another tray of honey biscuits out and rests it on top of the stove.

There's a tone to her voice I've not heard before—a mix of curiosity and concern. In an attempt to avoid scrutiny, I busy myself by washing the bowl, splashing water and forming bubbles. I don't want to lie, but it's the best for everyone at this point if I do. Just keep it close to my chest. There's a lot of shit going down, threats being made, and the last thing I want is for Mum or Dad to worry. 'Fine, demanding, tiring, cranky kids, frazzled parents. You know how it is this time of the year. Glad I could get a few days' leave, along with the public holidays, to come home.'

'Hmmm.'

When I turn around, Mum is leaning against the bench, arms crossed. I know this stance. This is her you-can't-pull-the-wool-over-my-eyes stance. The one I often saw during those last few years of school.

'What?' After wiping my hands, I mirror her stance. *Stick to your story, Scarlett.*

Mum tips her head to the side. I do the same. It's childish.

'Is this how you're going to play it?' Mum walks over to the answering machine (I'm still not sure why they have one when no one rings the home phone anymore) and presses a button.

'Hello, um, Mr and Mrs Reynolds. Sorry to bother you. My name is Stephanie, the owner and director of Gum Creek ELC in Adelaide. We're trying to get hold of Scarlett without much luck.' There's a pause with paper shuffling. Her voice is as nice as pie and I want to reach through the machine and do something unsavoury to her. 'Scarlett finished up unexpectedly, and we need to finalise her employment and some other matters that have come to hand. Can you please get her to call ASAP. Thank you, and Merry Christmas.'

Shit, shit, shit. Damn you, Stephanie, for dropping me right into it. And how dare she bring up the other issue in a message?

When I meet Mum's eyes, they are glassy. Her bottom lip trembles. This isn't the reaction I was expecting. I'd predicted disappointment, questions and concern. A lump forms in my throat; swallowing it is hard.

'Oh, Mum.' I fall into her outstretched arms. 'I'm sorry.'

'Why are you sorry, dear? You love what you do, and I know you wouldn't have quit unless you had a good reason to. You're a determined little bugger.' She sniffs in my ear.

I pull back and grab her some tissues from the box on the windowsill. 'Why are you crying then?'

'Because you're home for Christmas. Because we can finally spend time together. To chat about stuff and life and your job that you no longer have and what your plans are. And there's no rush for you to go back to the city now. Maybe you could do some day care here in Point Perry for a while. So many families would benefit.' She squeezes my hand, then presses the tissues to her eyes.

'No, Mum. My life's in the city. I have appointments, commitments. I can't stay here. Everything will work out, I promise.' I send her a smile, though it feels forced and tight. God, I hope everything does work out. The 'other matters' Stephanie referred to could get messy, but I need to see it through.

'Well, you can stay here as long as you need and keep me company. I've missed you an awful lot since your brothers moved out and started their families and it's just been your dad and me out here on the farm.'

It hits me. Mum's lonely. And although Dad is 'officially' retired, he still gets up and goes to work on the farm, doing whatever my other older brother Pete tells him to do. From sunup to sundown most days. And although the farm is only fifteen minutes from town, Mum never really talks about spending time there doing anything with friends other than catching up with Marge and Greta for a coffee every Thursday when she does the grocery shopping.

Guilt piles on me. Guilt about not being home during the last five years, for letting our relationship become a quick phone call every few weeks and the occasional text.

'So, you're crying happy tears that I quit my job and came home?'

She nods and swipes a tear from her cheek, leaving a floury streak. 'I know it's selfish, and I have a million questions, and I don't want to pressure you, but ...'

She's going to beg me to stay. Right now, my head is a jumble, and all my plans to keep this from my parents have gone out of the window. I have nothing to hide behind.

'How about I whip up a batch of Reynolds' Family Recipe Eggnog, pop on the carols and I'll fill you in?' I have a knack for always finding a way to shift the focus away from the current subject.

'I'd love that. Let me turn the oven off.'

When I turn back to the counter, bowl in one hand and a dozen eggs in the other, a pair of lights flicker up the dirt driveway.

'You expecting visitors, Mum?'

CHAPTER 7

Ryan

There is no missing the Reynolds' farm from the highway. It's lit up like a beacon. The arch over the cattle grid main gate is covered in—I slow and poke my head out the window—bloody mistletoe, with twinkling fairy lights that are flashing on and off in blue, green and red. Really?

If only my parents had thought to hang up a strand of twinkling lights. It could've made a difference. I push those thoughts to the back of my mind as I navigate the potholed dirt road taking me to the house.

Up ahead, the homestead glows with festive lights: reindeers, a sled, a dancing Santa, candy canes, spinning wheels, igloos, snowflakes, snowmen. Running across the front fence in LED lights is a train and some carriages. There is not a single surface that isn't twinkling. But the pièce de résistance is a massive blow-up Santa that towers on the house roof. And thank God the northerly wind has dropped, or it would be in Antarctica.

The temptation to do a U-turn and head back to town, to get as far away as possible from this ridiculous cheer, tugs at me. But I recall what Lilac said. Scarlett is only home for a week. Surely, we can be civil for that short amount of time, and then things will go back to normal when she returns to the city. Life will continue, Christmas will be over, and I can settle into my relatively new job and do the community thing.

After all, I'm only here to drop off the folder. That's all I'm required to do. Then I can get back to work and finish my shift. Five minutes, max. No discussion needed. No questions asked. Maybe I can just leave it on the front porch.

That thought is squashed when the front door swings open and a sucker punch strikes me square in the chest. Scarlett has covered the 'I'm too hot for Christmas' tee with a sexy Mrs Claus apron. I gulp a few mouthfuls of water from my bottle. Lick my lips.

Maybe Christmas isn't so bad after all.

I shake that thought from my head. There is nothing that could make this horrid period any better. I suck in a deep breath and open the car door, stepping out just as Scarlett marches down the path, bringing with her a waft of spices and baking.

'What brings you out to the farm, Nurse Ryan? No patients for you to see here, and quick, you'd better get back in your car before the Christmas lights grow tentacles and latch onto your arms.' Under her breath, it sounds like she adds, 'Grinch', but I can't be sure.

'You would be correct,' I snap and shove the folder against Mrs Claus' cleavage on the apron. 'I have no patience—for you, that is—and now you have this folder, I can get back into my car and leave you to it.'

And I do just that as her mouth forms an O, poised to say something, probably Christmas related because that's all she seems capable of.

The front screen door opens again, and an older woman with similar features to Scarlett hurries down the path and stands beside her. The apron forces me into smiling, and I wonder if inappropriate Christmas aprons are their family tradition.

I wouldn't know; I don't have any. Traditions or family who truly loved me. That familiar stab to the chest returns. The one that reminds me of everything I didn't have growing up, of everything I always wanted.

'Hello. Going by your name tag, you must be the infamous Ryan who is sending my Lettie into a spin.'

Scarlett shoves her mother's shoulder—assuming she is Mrs Reynolds—and growls, 'Mum,' between her teeth.

I hold my hand out. 'I'm Ryan Black. Lovely to meet you.'

She wipes her hands down her naked-man apron. 'I'm Rae, Lettie's mum. You're just in time; we're about to make our famous eggnog. Come into the cool and join us. You don't mind, do you, dear?' A knowing glance passes between Rae and Scarlett.

By the look on Scarlett's face, she one hundred percent does mind, and against my better judgement, and maybe more to the point, to annoy her further, I agree.

As I step around Scarlett, she mutters, 'By the way, was that a smile I saw earlier? You like the aprons? Perhaps I'm breaking your grinchiness.'

I shrug nonchalantly, not wanting to admit she could be right.

But that doesn't last long. When I thought it couldn't get more Christmassy, it does—just by entering the house. It's like stepping into the Christmas decoration section of a department store, where every nook and cranny, shelf and wall space has something Christmassy on it. It hits me, suffocates me.

It's totally foreign, and I'm glued to the floor, my mouth hanging open. So, this is what a family home looks like fully decked out for the festive season.

The real pine Christmas tree, which stands well over six

feet, is perched in the corner of the open-plan living area opposite the kitchen. Gifts of all shapes and sizes, wrapped in bright and colourful wrapping paper, are stacked high and wide on the floor underneath and surrounding the tree. And, of course, there are flashing lights wound around the tree from top to bottom. Twinkling like the night sky.

The beacon atop the tree draws me closer.

Stepping over the dog, who barely lifts its chin in greeting, around some shopping bags, and careful not to step on the presents, I peer up at the golden angel, her arms out wide. It's like she's welcoming me, beckoning me to let my guard down and open my heart to the possibilities of the joy this time of year brings.

A hand rests on my shoulder. Is it the devil about to tell me to ignore the angel? To remember past Christmases when there was no cheer? Or being told I was too old for presents, that I didn't deserve them?

When a warmth seeps through my shirt and trickles down my arm, I turn. No devil in sight, only the delectable Scarlett with a worried frown etched between her eyebrows.

When our eyes meet, a thousand questions are flicking through hers. She's studying me intently, as though trying to decipher my thoughts. No doubt trying to understand how the lanky teenager and the grumpy grinch are one and the same.

When my chest tightens and a bead of sweat forms across my temple, I know my time is up. Overwhelm catches in my throat, and a cough doesn't clear it.

'I ... I need to get some fresh air, get back to work ... Can't be ...' Shit, what is wrong with me? I can't even string a coherent sentence together.

Scarlett takes my hand in hers, and together, we navigate the obstacle course back to the front door, where she calls to

Rae, 'Mum, can you bring me that box? We'll be out on the swing.'

Then we're outside around the side of the house, where she grabs a camp lantern, turns it on, and leads me across the lawn to a giant double-seat swing hanging from a massive tree. She's holding my hand with such force it's almost painful. It's like she doesn't want to let me go. Let me go back to that dark place.

With the fairy lights gently twinkling through the branches, making it hard to see where the tree ends and where the clear night sky starts, it's less Christmassy and more romantic. As my anxiety starts to subside and the comforting warmth of Scarlett's hand soothes me, I can only hope to God she doesn't ask about what just happened as I'm not ready to share my story just yet.

CHAPTER 8

Scarlett

Hopefully, removing Ryan from the onslaught of Christmas in our house will give him some space to breathe and ground himself. The way his shoulders had tensed and the palpable tension radiating from his posture gave me a sneak peek into the turmoil of what this time brings for him. The pain in his eyes spoke volumes, but it was his visible relief when I guided him away that suggests there's more than just a stubborn grinchiness hidden behind that handsome veneer.

'Thank you.' His voice is barely a whisper above the gentle rustle of the leaves.

'I'm sorry,' I say at the same time, placing the lantern on the rustic table Dad made from an old jetty plank. 'I didn't ... shouldn't—'

'What are you apologising for? You weren't to know I'd ...' A huge sigh escapes him, and he shakes his head as if to clear the image.

'I just don't want you to think I did that on purpose ... as a joke.'

'No, no. It's okay. I'm good.'

There's no further discussion on the matter, and we settle on the swing. The well-worn rope is smooth against my palms. There's a distant bleating from the sheep. As I tuck my feet up on the seat, Ryan keeps his down and uses them to sway us back and forth, creating a gentle rock.

The silence is comfortable, surprisingly, even though there's a massive elephant in the room. I have so many questions, but I get a vibe from Ryan that he's processing. Hopefully, the quiet will allow him the space to do it.

'Here you go, love.' Mum wanders over to the swing, and I take the plastic jug and cups from the top of the box before they topple off. Ryan takes the box and settles it between us on the seat.

After thanking her and pouring us a drink, I lift the box lid, take out the wad of letters and hand them to Ryan. It might be a bit petty, but I need him to see the letters returned, to see that I held up my end of the deal and he didn't. Maybe I just need to show him I was right and justified in my anger.

'What are these?' There's an adorable crinkle around his eyes as he unties the ribbon, clearly trying to decipher what I've given him. It's almost my undoing. He taps the top letter. 'This is my handwriting.' The start of a smile shifts his lips. 'You kept them all?'

When he looks at me, his eyes are full of wonder. My stomach drops. Something isn't adding up. The anger that was simmering about these bloody letters starts to dissipate.

'All of them?' There's a hint of unintentional snide in my tone. 'I kept the one and only letter you sent. That one there on the top of the pile. Look at the others.'

His eyes quickly shift their focus back to the others in the pile. He transfers the first one to his left hand and sees my handwriting with 'return to sender' in red ink across the envelope, then he shuffles through the rest and blanches. When his hands start shaking, my heart squeezes. His jaw clenches; his shoulders stiffen. Then his hands grip the letters. Almost like he's trying to screw them up.

I drop the box to the ground and shuffle closer, laying my hands over his, willing them to relax, open. Now is not the time for me to get on my high horse about his lack of letter writing. I expected a tonne of excuses or for him to laugh off my over-the-top reaction, but what I get in return is an overwhelming display of raw emotions. Anger? Frustration? Defeat? They all play out in his facial expressions, his body language. There's more at play here. More than just a whirlwind of emotions from a brief summer romance and making promises to be pen pals.

'Talk to me, Ryan. What's going on?' I gently slide my finger along his rough jawline, hoping to ease the strain that lingers.

'I can't believe they did it.' His voice is tight, controlled. Finally, he releases the tension in his hands and gently flattens the envelopes on his lap.

'They? Who? Did what?' My mind races with countless scenarios, but I struggle to find a single plausible conclusion.

'My parents. They sent them all back to you.' He holds up the one addressed to me. 'Is this the only one you received?'

Confused and not sure what his parents have to do with this, I pinch my lips together and nod.

'It all makes sense now.' Despite growling the words out, there's a hint of sadness and acceptance in his tone.

'What makes sense? I'm not following.' I rest my palm on his forearm. 'Tell me what this is about, Ryan. Help me understand. Does this have something to do with your grinchiness?'

There's half a smile. 'Is that a made-up word?'

'It is, but let's get back on topic.'

He looks at the stars and releases the biggest sigh, then shuffles the letters. 'It's a long story. Have you got time?'

'Sure. Nowhere to be until choir practice tomorrow morning.'

He pushes again with one foot, and the swing gently sways forwards and backwards. 'My parents—who were my foster parents at the time—owned a post office. And it seems they intercepted your letters and returned them to you. It seems they also never sent the ones I gave them to post to you. Six months' worth. There's nothing worse than being lied to.'

Our gazes meet. Anger is simmering deep in my gut. Who would do that? And lies ... 'Oh, Ryan.'

There's so much pain and sorrow in his eyes that it makes my heart squeeze.

He slowly shakes his head; his chin drops to his chest. 'I'm sorry. I thought you were getting my letters but not replying. So eventually, I stopped writing.'

'And I assumed after this letter'—I tap the one he sent that's sitting on his leg—'even though you said to keep writing, that you were just leading me on. I was so angry at you when my next letter came back.'

It's my turn to suck in a deep breath and release it. Despite the passage of time, the anger and pain still linger within me. At the time, I'd thought we had a great relationship, albeit a long-distance one. As people would say nowadays: we had a 'connection'.

'I apologise for having a go at you earlier today.' For some reason, I don't want to remove my hand from his arm. The skin-on-skin connection is sending lovely little tingles through my fingers.

'And I apologise, too, for jumping to conclusions.'

'Seems your parents have some explaining to do.' I mean, who does that?

Ryan lets out a disgruntled huff. 'Not likely.' When his shoulders relent and slump, he continues, 'I was born on Christmas Day ... the same day I became a ward of the state.'

I suck in a sharp breath and hold it. When he gives me a sad smile, I release my breath. The smile is so familiar, and it makes me think back to the few smiles he gave me all those summers ago. He wasn't happy then either. My heart breaks a little more.

'My childhood wasn't that great. My foster parents weren't perfect, to say the least. I was yelled at often, sometimes hit, bullied. I had a few different homes. My birthday was always forgotten or overlooked because of Christmas. And Christmases were hard. My parents were strict. As I got older and found out they weren't my real parents, it was easier to despise them. When I look back, I can see they were self-absorbed. They made me think they were doing everything for me, but they were just doing things to stroke their egos.

'After that summer, I spent one more year at home, then, as soon as I turned eighteen, I left, and it's been just me ever since. I put myself through uni and have worked in Darwin and Perth to be away from the bad memories. And then I jumped at the chance to come back to Point Perry as there were good memories from here, even if at the time I was still pissy you didn't write.'

I press one hand against my heart, the other still on his arm, now squeezing. 'Thank you for trusting me with your story. That's some big and heavy stuff you've had to deal with, and there's so much to unpack. So many things I want to ask.'

Thump, thump goes my heart.

I scoot closer still. Ryan grounds his foot in the lawn, and the swing comes to a halt. My hands move instinctively to his cheeks; our eyes connect, then Ryan's dip and linger on my lips. A surge of longing for the carefree summer days builds deep in my stomach.

I'm unsure who makes the first move. A mere split second passes before our lips come into contact, lightly grazing and then pressing together. Heat flushes my cheeks, my core. His lips are soft before opening. My teeth scrape along his bottom lip. His stubble roughs my chin, sends tingles down my spine. A groan fills the still night. From me or him, I'm not sure.

Our chests collide, his breathing heavy, mine mirroring his rhythm. One of Ryan's hands slides under my top, up my spine to rest at the nape of my neck; the other tucks into the back waistband of my shorts.

I pull his head closer, running my fingers through his hair. Our tongues dance, slide and twirl. And his smell, salty from the wind and sweet from the bombardment of the baking in the kitchen. Home.

Home. But this isn't home. My life's in Adelaide, even though I no longer have a job. I have a career I need to keep building, unfinished business, obligations.

Abruptly, I pull away, my hands falling to my lap. I slide back to the edge of the swing, creating much-needed distance between us.

'I'm sorry, Ryan. That wasn't meant to happen. Shit.' At his stunned and somewhat confused look, I continue, 'I'm only back for a few days. It's not fair on either of us to start something that can't be finished, so to speak.'

Ryan stands and straightens his scrubs. 'Yeah, sure. No worries. I have to get back to work anyway and let Lilac know the folder has been handed over safely.' He tosses the envelopes onto the top of the box. 'I'll catch you around, then.'

I reach for his hand, but he shrugs away. 'Wait, please.'

As Ryan walks back to his car, the honey biscuits I scoffed earlier threaten to reappear. I'm such a shitty person for doing that. He trusted me with his story, and then I turned him away. I'm just another person who's disappointed him. And it doesn't sit well at all.

Ryan deserves someone who's going to stick around for the long haul, and that's not me.

CHAPTER 9

Ryan

Despite not drinking any alcohol last night, my head pounds like I have a hangover. When I went back to check on Lilac, who grilled me about what happened—I swear she has a sixth sense—I provided her with the bare minimum details: met Rae, sorted communication issues with Scarlett, delivered the folder as requested. No way was I going to tell her about my confession or 'the kiss'. The kiss that kept me tossing and turning most of the night, along with flashbacks of teenage romps in the back of a Sandman, kisses that were perfect then ... and now.

Clicking fingers in front of my eyes startles me.

'You right there, mate?' Larry is behind the Perry's Café counter, hands braced on the edge of it, eyebrows raised. 'You look like you could use one of these'—he pats the coffee machine—'and a piece of Marge's carrot cake.'

'You, Larry, are reading my mind. Both to go, please.' I hand over my trusty yellow reusable coffee cup and tap my phone on the EFT device. 'You by yourself this morning? Where's Marge?'

Larry rolls his eyes. 'My lovely wife and Greta are knee-deep in getting things set up for the markets and the Lighting of the Jetty. The joys of having your own business—you can come and go as you need. Although, Marge had some sniffles this morning, so hopefully, she's taking it easy.' He looks me up and down. 'No scrubs? Day off?'

An unsettling feeling tugs at the pit of my stomach. Larry is about to—

'I could use a hand with the lights if you have some spare time? Marge's been nagging me to get them done, and with the weather much nicer today, she's instructed me that today's the day. And considering the lighting is only two days away, it'll give us time to make sure they work and change any globes that've blown.'

Yep, called it.

'You'd be doing me a massive favour, Ryan.'

As much as I want nothing to do with anything associated with the Christmas spectacle, I also can't say no. It isn't in my DNA. I'm a helper at heart, which is what led me to nursing. And how Christmassy can hanging lights on the jetty be? It certainly won't be anything like the Reynolds' farm, that's for sure. And I'm sure a certain singer won't be anywhere near the jetty today, according to Lilac's itinerary for Scarlett, which I may have sneaked a peek at last night.

'No probs at all. I don't have any plans that can't be moved to tomorrow.'

'Great!' Larry looks at his watch. 'Can you swing by the town hall and pick up the lights? Councillor Giles said they're in the storeroom. A few of us are meeting at the jetty in half an hour. Marge will be back by then, and I can scoot off and meet you down there.'

Hmm. The town hall ... that's where the itinerary said Scarlett *would* be this morning. But surely, I can get to the storeroom from a side entrance and avoid an awkward encounter. I've promised Larry and can't back out now. 'Will do. I'll chuck my ladder in, too.'

'You're a lifesaver.' Larry chuckles. 'Quite literally, according to Lilac.' He hands over my coffee, and I scrunch the top of the paper bag to carry the cake. 'See you soon.'

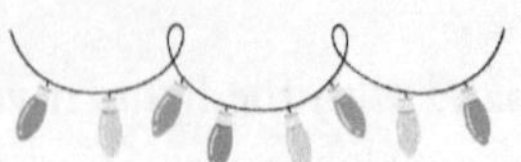

The singing of the less-than-perfect-sounding choir smacks me in the face as I cross the town hall foyer in search of the storeroom, which is nowhere to be found.

As I discretely peek into the hall, it's a scene of complete and utter chaos. What looks to be an out-of-control creche is set up in the back corner of the hall. Plastic toys, books and prams are spread out with babies lying on blankets, toddlers smacking each other with blocks and one child having a tantrum. A couple of older toddlers are scooting around on pedal-less bikes, coming close to running into some choir members from Seaside Village sitting in wheelchairs in front of the stage.

Sneaking in, I make my way towards the double doors on the side of the hall, confident that's where I'll find the storeroom.

'Hello, Nurse Ryan.' Ingrid holds up a shaky hand, waving gold tinsel around. 'Have you come to join the choir with our lovely Scarlett? She truly is an angel.'

So much for coming in unnoticed. I send her my best smile. 'You don't want to hear me sing, Ingrid. I'm terrible. I'll leave it to you. You sound great. I could hear you from down the street.'

'Well, aren't you just the kindest.'

'Ingrid, is the storeroom through here?' I point to the door. 'Just grabbing the jetty lights for Larry.'

'Yes, dear, go through that door, then through the kitchen. Storeroom is on the left, just down the corridor. So glad you're helping with the lights. It's such a lovely time of the year, don't you think?'

'Just great,' I say through clenched teeth, throwing a wave over my shoulder as I head towards the kitchen. The sooner I get what I came for and get out of here, the better.

A yellow stream of light is coming out of what I assume is the storeroom, with the door slightly ajar. As I get closer, an unmistakable voice rises above the commotion in the hall.

'Stephanie, there is no way I will be returning to any of your childcare centres while you have anything to do with them. I don't want to be associated with you in any way or form. Please do not contact me again.'

The speaking stops for a moment.

'I can no longer remain silent about your narcissistic bullying; you're a horrible person, and I refuse to continue sweeping your behaviour under the carpet. The authorities are investigating you, and it won't be long until word gets around about your shoddy businesses, and you'll be left with nothing.'

I don't want to eavesdrop or invade her privacy, so I linger in the kitchen, looking out the window at the metal Santa sleigh mounted on the roof of the auto mechanic shop and the posters for the Find a Grinch competition. Is someone playing a joke on me?

After what seems like ages of no further speaking, and assuming Scarlett has left via the exit at the other end of the corridor, I push the door open and step into the room. There are boxes of 'stuff' along one wall and what looks to be theatre props leaning against another. Spinning around to see what else is here, and hoping to find a box that says 'jetty lights', I find Scarlett sitting in the corner, knees pulled to her chest, head resting on top of them, Santa hat flopped forward.

'Hey.' I gently place my hand on her arm so as not to startle her.

When she lifts her head, there's a tinkle from her bell earrings. I can't read her face, though. I'm not sure if she's angry or frustrated. She looks to be just totally over it. Whatever 'it' is. All her Christmassy joy has vanished, and this tugs at my heartstrings. Which leaves me bewildered, confused. But why? For all my hangups about Christmas, I'd rather see her festive cheer and over-the-topness than this woman who appears defeated.

I squat in front of her. 'I kind of overheard some of that conversation. It sounded pretty intense. Is everything okay? You want to talk about it?'

When she relents with a slight nod, I sit on the grubby carpet and cross my legs.

'Stephanie is the owner of a childcare centre I was working for. I quit.' She sucks in a deep breath. 'I've reported her to the Education Standards Board, and she's being investigated, which is why I need to head back to Adelaide ASAP. I also have the small matter of finding another job and a mortgage to pay.'

'And bullying? What's that all about?'

'You heard that?'

When I nod, she takes a while before she answers. It's like she's hiding something or contemplating her answer. Is there something more to her story? Is there a greater threat?

'Everything's okay.' Scarlett quickly stands up and dusts herself off.

She reaches her hand to me, and I take it. Is that a little spark? As she pulls, I untangle my legs and stand. There's barely an inch between us. Her chest heaves. My heart pounds. Her gaze lands on my mouth.

'And that's not the worst of it,' she mutters, her eyes flicking up to mine, a flash of cheekiness in them.

'It's not?'

'No.'

'What's the worst thing, then?'

She slips her hand out of mine and clasps both of hers around my neck. 'The worst thing is I want to kiss you again—'

'And that's a problem because ...?' I nuzzle my nose behind her ear. Hmm ... cinnamon and lemon.

'I can't start something I can't finish. I don't want a five-day fling ...'

'Like when we were seventeen?' Our bodies are flush now. Heat radiates from where we join. My arms slide around her waist and rest at the top of her butt. She has a point. Can I start this only to see her leave? Déjà vu. 'Can you stay a little bit longer?'

Why did I ask that? That'd only be delaying the inevitable.

'Ah, here you are. We were just about to send a search party out for both of you.' Greta—aka Gossiping Greta—stands in the doorway, hands on her slim, sixty-something-year-old hips. 'Now we know where you are, I'll leave you to ... whatever you were doing. As you were.' She nods, does an about-face and is gone, no doubt to share the news of our compromising position, which will be around town before you can sing 'Silent Night'. *Great.*

Interestingly, though, neither of us moved a millimetre while Greta was in the doorway. From my perspective, I didn't want to let Scarlett go. She felt too comfortable pressed against me. Like we were two pieces of a jigsaw puzzle that had finally found where they needed to be. The irony.

There's no time to ponder this revelation as Scarlett's lips are against mine. Hard. She moans; I growl. Her hands tug at the hair at the back of my head. My hands press her butt, forcing her hips into my erection. Then her hands move to my chest, and she pushes me until my back slams into a stack of boxes. They move, wobble. My balance is lost. The boxes topple. We stumble and end up on our backs, panting.

Scarlett starts giggling first as she sits. I follow suit, standing and adjusting myself before reaching out to pull her up.

'I'm sorry, Ryan. I totally jumped you then.' Her giggles subside. 'Not sure what came over me.'

'I'm totally on board with you jumping me.' I can't help but smile at the flush on her cheeks and the Santa hat that's slipped to the side of her head.

'But we need to finish that conversation from before when we're not deep in Christmas stuff.' She tilts her head to the door. A cacophony of screeching, squealing, crying and out-of-tune singing makes its way down to the storeroom. 'And by the sound of what's coming from the hall, I'd better get back and instil some order.'

'And I better find the jetty lights before Larry hunts me down, and I want to pop in and say hello to Lilac, too.'

Her hands rest on my cheeks. 'Tell Lilac I said hello and that everything is under control. And do you want to catch up later?'

'Sure, that'd be great. Here'—I pull my phone from my shorts pocket, unlock it and hand it over. 'Pop your number in and I'll text you my address.'

When she's finished, she hands it back to me, leans in for another sweet kiss on my lips, and then confidently strolls through the door, playfully flicking the bell on her hat over her shoulder, leaving me shaking my head with a silly grin on my face.

Is it too much to hope Scarlett will light up my heart this Christmas? Not sure I can survive her walking away from me again.

CHAPTER 10

Scarlett

Ah, great. Not only have I lied to Ryan's face, but I've also stepped back into the hall to find Greta in her element. You'd think after the scandal she was embroiled in last year that she would've changed. But, no, Gossiping Greta is holding court in front of the hall's stage and the mention of my name, along with Ryan's, is undeniable. There are ooohs and aahhhs and a few comments such as: he's an absolute catch, I'd love to pash him (this one from Ingrid, bless her eighty-six-year-old heart), and it's a Christmas miracle. But ... there will be no miracle as I won't be staying in Point Perry.

'Ouch!' Two bike wheels run over my open-toed slip-ons. Cursing under my breath, I grab the back of the rider's tee and, with my other hand, grab the handlebars, bringing the bike to a halt. I squat. 'Hey, Evie, how about you hop off your bike as the way you're riding it in the hall is a bit dangerous?'

Two big, round, piercing blue eyes stare back at me. Her bottom lip wobbles. There's the faintest of nods. 'Sorry, Aunty Lettie. I didn't mean to run over you.'

'We don't want any more accidents, and you don't want to hurt yourself either by crashing.' I quickly scan the hall for my sister-in-law, Justine.

'She's just gone to the loo,' someone calls.

'How about we set you up with another activity?' I ask my niece and receive another nod in exchange. 'Would you like a piggyback?' Another nod.

Once she's climbed onto my back and all but strangled me with her arms, I skip over to the hall corner—eliciting giggles —where the makeshift creche has been set up. As she slides down my back like a slippery dip, she tickles me under my ribs, the little bugger, and it's just the cutest thing. It's so cute that I exaggerate my laughing and fall to the floor, pulling Evie with me. Then it's an all-in pile-on tickle fest with the other half a dozen kids who swarm in like flies.

And for a few minutes, nothing else seems to matter. Not the fact I have no job or that I'm starting to fall for a guy ... who I'll be walking away from in less than a week.

I catch sight of Ryan leaning against the foyer doorway, his legs crossed at the ankles and his arms full of boxes brimming with light bulbs and electrical cords. The expression on his face is a sight to behold.

A smile reaches from ear to ear, and it's not one of those wincey, half-try-hard smiles. But one that lights his entire face. Laugh lines crinkle out from his eyes, and he nods, a knowing nod that says: you look right at home.

Something slams into my chest. I'd like to think it's a child's elbow or knee, but it isn't.

Whatever it is, I want to keep feeling it if it means I'll keep seeing that smile. I will tell him about the last six months of my job, the mental load, the therapy. Lay it all on the table.

As he pushes off the doorframe, he awkwardly waves his hand from under the box before disappearing.

'Okay, you lot, up and off me, please.' I gently push bodies to the floor amid more tickles and squeals. 'Let's get you busy with something else while the grownups are finishing their singing.'

'Can you play with us too, Aunty Lettie?' Evie's cheeks are flushed from the wrestling match.

To be honest, hanging out with the under-fives sounds like more fun than wrangling out-of-tune locals into something that resembles a choir. But I can't let Lilac down.

'Pleeeaaase?' Evie pulls me over to a large wooden box in the corner where the creche is set up. 'What can we do?'

'Well, just give me a minute, sweety.' I turn to face Greta, Ingrid and the rest of the choir who are all still huddled together. 'Point Perry Choir members,' I call, 'back to your places, please. Let's do one more run-through of "The Twelve Days of Christmas" with the changes I made earlier. Graham, remember to come in lower on the partridge in a pear tree, and Verity, try and take the five golden rings a touch higher. Everyone else, just try and stay in tune, and remember I'm soloing the last verse just as Lilac was, okay?'

There are nods, foot shuffles and murmurings as everyone takes their places. On my count of three, Greta presses play on the music system and off they go.

'Now, Miss Evie, what are your friends' names?' The kids have my full attention now as I block out the choir and ... oh dear ... there goes Mabel's screeching.

Evie goes around the circle. 'This is Asha, Ned, Kya, Bella and Remy. They are all my friends.' She slings an arm around Remy, who is wearing the most adorable red tutu with tiny gold bells that tinkle every time she moves. If only they made it in adult sizes.

'Okay, let's see what's in this box.' Rummaging around, I find a bundle of hula hoops, some hacky sacks, a bucket of chalk and three frisbees—not ideal inside toys. Hoisting the hoops out, I ask the kids to grab a sack each.

'Follow me, troops.' They fall into line behind me as I march away from the choir. When I stop suddenly, they all bang into me and each other, causing another raucous round of giggles. 'Listen up. Who can stay the stillest while I set the game up? No one can move.'

'Can we talk?' Ned swipes at a piece of hair hanging over his eyes.

'No. You have to be as quiet as a mouse.' I place the hoops out in a hopscotch pattern, stopping and twisting with exaggeration after each hoop to check if anyone is moving or talking ... causing more giggles. Just as I place the final hoop, someone farts, and, well, that's it. The entire population in the hall, choir included, loses the plot and erupts into mayhem.

Someone bumps into my shoulder before skirting their arm around my waist. 'You are so good with the kids, Scarlett. It's a shame you're heading back to Adelaide as Point Perry desperately needs day care or a new childcare centre.' Justine smiles and shakes her head as the kids all pinch their noses, and the choir clamours out the side door for some fresh air.

First Mum's suggestion of day care and now Justine's. Is it an option? Could I do it? Not with my paltry savings and a mortgage, no bank will loan me the cash, and starting up a new business isn't cheap with securing a location, insurance, marketing and supplies. And do I want to put myself through more stress so soon? I chew on my bottom lip as scenarios flash through my brain.

Then, clarity hits me like a wrecking ball.

Turning, I clasp Justine's cheeks between my hands, and a buzz of excitement vibrates through me. 'Actually, Justine, I think you've just delivered the best Christmas gift a girl could ask for.'

She looks at me with raised brows. 'Oh?'

'I need to fill you in; it's not common knowledge. I only told Mum yesterday, but I quit my job in Adelaide last week.

And you've just planted a seed of hope.' I pull her into a bear hug—the Rudolph nose on her tee squeaking as we press together—and whisper my thanks in her ear.

However, can I abandon my city lifestyle completely, or will my demons follow me home to Point Perry?

CHAPTER 11

Ryan

'How's my favourite nurse today?' Seated by the window, Lilac overlooks the jetty and bay from her recliner chair. 'Doc said I need another day in here just to check a few more things and make sure the head and arm are as good as can be. Then I have to spend some time in respite in Seaside Village. And I told him in no uncertain terms there's no way in hell I'm going there when I can look after myself in the comfort of my home like I have been for the last sixty-five years. I even promised to consider Meals on Wheels.'

When she takes a breath, I open my mouth to reply, but she beats me to it.

'Now, Larry called in to update me on the jetty lights and mentioned you were helping, but there's not much action down there. They need a bit of a razz up. And thank you for delivering the choir folder to Scarlett. She also visited earlier this morning, returned my rings, all cleaned and polished. Bless her heart. She's a fine, young, capable lady, don't you think? Full of beans, and she had a spring in her step today.'

My mouth opens again ... Nope, not going to get a word in.

'And I must say, at the mention of your name, those sweet cheeks of hers turned a delightful shade of watermelon.' A knowing smirk tugs at her lips. 'Kind of like the colour yours are right now under that scruff on your face.'

I chuckle. 'It's rather hot outside, is all. And I had to rush from the hall to get here.'

'Hmm ... is that so?' She slurps some cordial through a straw. 'What's the update from the choir practice?'

Greta catching us in a compromising position means Lilac will inevitably find out—sooner rather than later—making the situation even worse. As I debate the pros and cons of telling Lilac, I ultimately decide to keep my mouth shut and face her scolding later when the grapevine reaches her.

Even though I'm off duty, I check Lilac's charts, running my eyes over her nightly obs. Thankfully, they all look good.

'The choir was sounding wonderful.'

She lets out a huff. 'Liar.'

I make my way over to the window and lean against the frame, watching a sleepy lizard sun itself on a granite boulder in the garden. 'Scarlett was trying her hardest to make them sound wonderful.'

'That's more like it.'

'In between wrangling kids and ...'

'... snogging in the storeroom.'

A cough catches in my throat, and I guzzle some water from the bottle I brought with me. Lilac is a straight shooter; maybe I can take a leaf from her book.

'That's right.' I straighten and wait for her next move.

'So that problem you had with her, it's all sorted now? Water under the bridge ... or jetty.' She waves her hand towards the window view.

'Well, yes, and no. It's ... complicated.'

She lets out an enormous sigh. 'I don't know. You young ones ...' Our gazes meet. 'Sit and tell me all about it.' She points to the spare visitor's chair in the corner. I pull it over and sit as told. 'It's only complicated if you make it. Kids today make everything hard when you just need to follow your heart. What's your heart saying?'

Instinctively, I rub the tightening behind my sternum. 'Hit me with the big question, why don't you, Lilac.' The bay sparkles a brilliant turquoise, boats are dotted on the water, and kids are jetty jumping. 'I like her, a lot, and often thought of her, even to the point of trying to find her on social media, without any luck.'

'But ... what is your head saying?'

'She's going back to Adelaide next week.'

'I believe she has no job to go back to, though,' Lilac states. When I frown, she adds, 'Scarlett's mother rang this morning to check if there's anything she can do to help and told me all about it.'

Poor Scarlett having her news blabbed around town, especially by her mum, when she's still trying to process it herself. 'That's right. She has no job and probably wouldn't be happy that the news is spreading around town like wildfire either. But there's nothing here for her, and she has a career and needs to pay the bills. She wants to go home, back to the city. Told me so just this morning.' This morning. Only twenty minutes ago, after she jumped me and left me hard but confused. Wanting more ... and then I saw her so happy, playing with the kids. 'So, what do you suggest I do, then?'

There's a twinkle in Lilac's eyes like she's up to no good, which would be right on the money for Lilac. 'Simple—make her stay. Oh, and while you're at it, see if you can find a way so I can stay in my home, too.' She taps her bottom lip. 'Maybe there's a job she can do. I can pay her.'

The cogs turn in my head, and I lean forward in the seat.

'Well, she is qualified to care for children'—I grin at her—'and change nappies and spoon feed.'

Lilac scoffs, picks up her walking stick resting against the recliner and pokes me in the stomach. 'You cheeky smartarse.' Her laugh is infectious, and it brings a lightness to my chest. It's a random feeling for this time of the year when I'm usually sullen and avoid people.

'It's good to see you laugh again, Ryan. Now, get your thinking cap on, get down to the jetty, get those lights hung and then go get your girl.'

I stand and salute. 'Yes, ma'am. Larry will be wondering where I've got to.'

'Get out of here!' She waves her cane towards the door.

After straightening her bed and refilling her jug with orange cordial, I rest a hand on her shoulder. 'I'll see what I can do about getting you home, okay? You happy for me to drop in and check what needs doing inside? Might need some more safety rails and handles.'

'Thank you, dear. I'd appreciate that. Just pop through the back door. Don't tell anyone, but I don't lock it.'

I tap my nose. 'Your secret's safe with me, Lilac.'

'I really don't want to go into the village. I know I can cope at home with a little help.' She pats my hand. 'Oh, can you grab that note next to the phone, please?' When I hand it over, she holds her hand up. 'It's a list of families doing it tough this year. Marge offered to do some hampers and get some toys for the kids. Can you get the list to her?'

'Sure, Lilac. Leave it with me. We'll get it all sorted. Now, you stay there in your comfy recliner while we do all the hard work.'

This elicits another cheeky grin, and I leave her room on a mission.

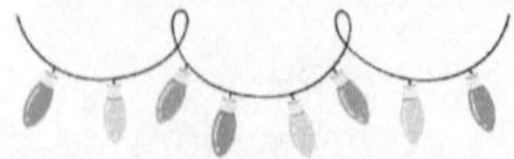

Perry's Café is jam-packed with a mix of locals and tourists, ordering coffees and brunches, and stocking up on bait, burley and last-minute Christmas essentials. But Marge is nowhere in sight, which is unusual for the café owner. I do a quick drive around town, past her house, the IGA, the hall, the school library, and there's still no sign of her.

As I pull into the only available parking space by the jetty, I'm met with a Christmas tree almost double my six-foot-seven height. The smell of pine lingers on the salty breeze. Memories of not having a Christmas tree during my child-hood resurface as they did when I stood in Scarlett's house, staring at her beautifully decorated tree. As the waves of simmering anger and spite recede, a newfound curiosity sparks within me.

A group of primary-school-aged kids are mucking around off to the side, trying to flick each other with their beach towels, with Tom—one of the schoolteachers I'd recently met when his pregnant wife came into the hospital for stitches in her foot—telling them off while waiting for some stragglers wandering down the hill towards the jetty.

'Hey, Tom.' I wave as I open the back of my wagon to grab the boxes of lights and pull out the multi-fold ladder. 'Do you know where your mum is by any chance?'

'She's in bed, crook with the flu or something.' Woody, his kelpie, sits at his feet, earning the dog an ear scratch. 'She must be bad to end up in bed.'

'Ah, damn. That's no good. Your dad did say she had the sniffles when I saw him this morning. She must've gone down-hill fast.'

Since both my arms are laden with the boxes of lights,

Tom jogs over and presses the button to close the boot. 'Yeah, she did. She's run herself ragged like she does this time every year, trying to help everyone else and make sure the community is looked after, forgetting to look after herself. We've all been trying to tell her to slow down and share the load ... delegate ... but now she has no choice. And with Lilac out of action too, there are a few more jobs for everyone else to pick up.'

'That there are. I'm starting to get the feeling that it's all hands on deck when an event is being organised in Point Perry, and it's great to see everyone rally around.'

'It sure is. Especially at Christmastime when the farmers have finished reaping, school's out and the tourists start arriving.'

'There sure is a buzz around town. I'll call past later and check in on Marge.'

'She'll love that.' Tom winks and turns back to the kids. Pointing to the ladder, he asks, 'Can we use that?'

'Sure can. Told Larry I'd bring an extra.'

Tom grabs the ladder and sets it up next to the tree. 'Okay, kids, let's get this tree decorated.'

With the two boxes of lights in my arms, I head down the jetty and find Larry onboard his crayfish and fishing charter boat *The Margaret,* along with a dozen or so locals, including Fabian and Jonesy who work for Larry, all enjoying a morning tea of Christmas cake and cups of coffee in enamel mugs. And I can't *not* notice the metres and metres of tinsel adorning the wheelhouse and deck area.

'About time!' Larry climbs the steps and stands on the jetty. 'We had to have a cuppa while we waited for you. And here'—he holds out his hand to the man who'd followed him onto the jetty—'let me introduce you to Jack Reynolds. Jack, this is young Ryan Black, new nurse up at the hospital.'

Shite. Well, this is awkward. He has to be Scarlett's father, with the same nose and coloured eyes ... I place the boxes on the jetty and outstretch my hand. Jack's is worn and calloused, no doubt from years of farm labour.

'Ah, you must be the Ryan who sent the ladies on my farm into a spin last night.' Jack's expression is straight, lips set.

'Um, yes. Lilac asked me to drop some things out to Scarlett, and I met Rae.'

Jack chuckles. 'God, I'm so sorry, mate, that you had to see all that.'

When I frown, he shakes his head. His face lights up with a hearty laugh, loud enough to scare some seagulls perched on the light post. 'All the Christmas stuff. Rae loves it, but with Lettie home this year, she's gone a bit ... what does my granddaughter say? Nek level.' He waves off the slang. 'Anyway, I've tried telling her to tone it down, but she won't listen. It's all rather embarrassing, but at least we're far enough out of town and don't get many visitors.' He slaps me on the back. 'Righto, let's get these lights up.'

Larry grabs the top box from the pile. 'Tell me again what took you so long?'

Unsure of what to make of Jack, I clear my throat and struggle to find the right words to reply about the abundance of Christmas decorations. 'No probs, Jack. And, Larry, I had a few detours. Checked in on Lilac and went searching for your wife. Bugger that she ended up in bed. Told Tom I'd check in on her later.'

'You're a good bloke. Thank you. Pretty sure it's just a cold and she'll be right as rain soon. Just means we'll be having a quiet Christmas, and she'll have to put her feet up and let us all look after her for a change.'

'That sounds like a good plan, Larry. Now, are you happy for me to leave the lights and duck off? I have a few errands to run, and it looks like you have a big team of helpers here to string them up, and Tom is sorted with the tree.'

'Yep, all good, mate. You go do what you need, and we'll see you back here for the lighting tomorrow night.'

'Sure. Looking forward to it.' And ... am I?

As I walk past the Christmas tree, Tom's son Carter—dressed as Buzz Lightyear (what a nice change from anything Christmas related)—grabs my hand, Woody close by. 'Ryan, come and look at the decorations we're hanging on the tree. We made them at school before the holidays started.'

He tugs me closer and again; I'm hit with the scents of pine and eucalyptus mixed with sand and brine. I rub a twig between my fingers and hold it to my nose, inhaling deeply. Is this the smell of Christmas? Not cigarette smoke, alcohol-laced breath and burnt sausages? I shake my head to dislodge the memories, trying to put them in a box and lock the lid, shove them to the back of my mind.

Hung around the lower branches of the tree by red ribbons are laminated name tags. Some have photos on the back; others have regiment names, hand-drawn pictures and messages.

One reads: Bryan Smyth—much loved by all. Another: Molly Fitzgerald, inscribed below a photo of a curly, blonde girl. And: Bartholomew R Andrews—1916 Light Horse Regiment.

'It's a memory tree.' Carter slips another name on a branch. 'Every year, we hang the names of people who've died. It's sad but happy too. That way, people in the town can remember others. And some of the people we talk about in class. Who they were and what they did in Point Perry.' For a six-year-old, he shows a lot of empathy. 'This one'—he holds up a laminated heart-shaped decoration with *Nanna Bee* scrawled on the front—'is my nanna. I never met her, but she taught Dad how to play the piano.'

There's that feeling in my chest again, behind my breastbone. I clear my throat. 'This is such a nice thing to do.' I grab a couple of names from the tub sitting on the sand and hang them higher, and while I'm there, I slip some giant red baubles on as well.

'And then tomorrow night, when we light up the jetty, we have candles too and sing carols. And'—his eyes go as wide as saucers—'Father Christmas comes, and we all get a present. Last year, he came on Gramps' boat. It was so much fun.'

'Wow! That is very cool.' What a great way to celebrate the past and ensure all the kids get something. I slip my hand into my shorts pocket. Lilac's list is still there, and I have to go shopping.

Hopefully, the few shops in Point Perry will have everything I need.

CHAPTER 12

Scarlett

Will this day ever end?

After wrangling children, choir members and a parking spot near the grocery store, plus being subjected to various comments about being sprung in the storeroom with Ryan and receiving a scathing text from Stephanie, and weaselling my way out of work in the service station, I end up in the cream-brick building on the main street housing the council chambers—more specifically, Councillor Giles' office.

When Mum had called with a list of things to get from the shops, she'd also let slip that she'd told Lilac about my out-of-work predicament. Not great—this news will be all over town before sundown. Lilac had said that Gossiping Greta had told her that at the last council meeting, there had been a heated debate about what to do with the donation of half a million dollars that Hanna Charlton—ex-Point Perry resident and now Hollywood movie star who'd returned home recently for the movie premiere of *Second Chance Love*—had made to the town of Point Perry.

When I'd told Mum about my idea to help the community, she'd cried, bless her. 'You're staying in Perry. My girl is coming home,' she'd wept before listing the prominent locals and surrounding businesspeople she'd call and table the proposal to, seeking the additional funding. Funding will be the biggest issue, and at this moment, there's not enough. With no bank branch in Point Perry, I called a friend of a friend in Adelaide who is a mortgage broker specialising in commercial loans. He pretty much said, as things stand, that my financials probably weren't strong enough, but he would look closer and see what he could do in the new year.

My hands are tied. I can't do anything about it.

The idea started brewing after Justine's comment in the hall and blossomed. I'd ducked into Perry's Café to grab a new non-Christmas tee, removed my Santa hat and bell earrings, and presented myself as a want-to-be business owner.

From the newsagent, I'd bought a notepad, pencil and eraser, all while churning the specifics over in my head. Numbers: dollars, population, children, supplies, wages and building costs all solidified, and over a coffee and slice of Marge's carrot cake, I'd scribbled a rough business plan.

Now, as I sit in Councillor Giles' office, my gaze instinctively shifts towards a stunning oil painting adorning the wall, capturing the essence of the local, rugged coastline. It reminds me of the pure bliss of being at one with Mother Nature. It ignites a desire within me to make this dream happen so I can enjoy it more.

My mouth is dry, and I wipe my sweaty palms on my shorts. His desk is sparse—only a pot of pens and a picture frame, presumably of his family—like he's packed it up for the holidays, and he's wearing casual clothes with an impatient look on his face.

'Scarlett Reynolds, what's so urgent it couldn't wait until the end of January? I'm technically on leave, and they are waiting for me down on the jetty to get those lights hung for tomorrow night.'

'Love.' The word escapes my mouth before I can stop it. And where did it come from? It isn't love for Ryan. I mean, I like him, but ... it must be love for my family, Point Perry, the community, the kids. Let's try again. 'I'd *love* a Christmas miracle for the community.'

Councillor Giles remains mute, eyebrows raised. 'I don't have time for tomfoolery.' He stands to leave, slinging his satchel over his shoulder.

My stomach drops, but I don't move an inch. I won't roll over that easily or quickly. 'I have a business proposal for a much-needed and wanted childcare centre to be built in Point Perry, partly funded by Hanna Charlton's donation, the remaining by private investors.' I slide my notebook across his polished wooden desk. 'All the information you need is in here, and apologies for the pencil. Or, if you want, I can type it up. But then you won't get it until after Christmas and, well, I'm keen to get things moving.'

Councillor Giles freezes in his tracks before retracing his steps back to his seat. Dropping his satchel on the floor and getting comfy in his chair, he pulls the notebook closer and opens the front page. My poor heart is going a million miles an hour as I sit on my hands to stop from picking at my nails.

I can picture it so clearly: a modern building with rooms for babies, toddlers and preschoolers. Lots of big windows and areas to be creative, to rest and to come together. Outside will be grass, interactive play equipment, nature, water and every parent's favourite—sand. And it will be affordable for everyone with qualified staff.

But most of all, I'll be back home with a job I love and in a centre I can run the way it should be ... how I want it to be. With the children's best interests at the forefront. Unlike a certain other centre and its director.

Councillor Giles clears his throat, flicks through the last few pages and closes my notepad. 'It's not possible, Scarlett. It's a no from me, and I'd think a no from the majority of the sitting members.'

My heart thuds to the ground. 'But—'

'This all looks unprofessional, and there are no detailed building quotes, only your generalised estimates. Which at first glance seems extremely low for rural build. There are other projects on the table for the donation and, to be honest, a childcare centre isn't high on the priority list.'

'But—'

Councillor Giles holds up a hand to stop me. 'I wouldn't go making any plans around it happening. In other words: continue as if it weren't to happen.'

Just as I'm about to argue, he gets up and puts the chair back under the table. If he's already dismissed my proposal, there's no way he's keeping my notepad, so I snatch it back with a mix of frustration and fury. I suppose it's to be expected two days before Christmas when everyone is already in holiday mode. But I won't give up. I won't back down on this new dream without pouring everything into it. There are other avenues, and a large portion of the community will back me. A community that will all be in one place tomorrow night for the Lighting of the Jetty.

'If you think childcare isn't a priority, I think you're very much out of touch with your community, Councillor Giles. It will happen; just you wait and see.'

Outside the council office, I call Mum and update her.

'Don't you worry, love. Dad and I'll put calls into the councillors to rally some support, and we can catch up with them and chat face-to-face at the jetty lightning. We'll tell them your plan and how it will positively impact the community. Don't give up.'

With an hour left before the choir is meeting at Seaside

Village, and with no time to go back to the farm to use the computer and printer and return to Point Perry, I hurriedly make my way to the school library, hoping it will still be open, even though school finished last week.

As I round the corner, I'm relieved to see the lights are on in the library and the street placard is still standing on the footpath. There's a bunch of gold star balloons bobbing in the breeze, which brings a smile to my face. Out front, a few dusty cars and farm utes are parked, reflecting how dry it's been.

The air conditioning is a welcome relief as I push the door open and find the librarian, a lovely Canadian guy who, after I've explained what I'm doing, points me to a computer and tells me he's in full support after seeing the need and listening to families who come in for some of the programs he offers.

I quickly type up the petition, send the file to print and wait impatiently by the printer. Other patrons meander through the aisles, their fingers tracing the spines of books as they read the back covers before deciding whether to return them to the shelf or take them home. The overhead lights flicker before going out, sending the library into a muted darkness as the sun disappears behind a cloud. The whirr of the air conditioner ceases. Terrible timing for a power outage. There's an eerie silence as if we're holding our breaths, not just for the power to come back on but for the petition outcome or for the council's decision.

A commotion at the door breaks the silence as the library patrons gather at the front desk, waiting to see if the power will return. The fact that it's a stinker of a day and it hasn't come back on straight away isn't a good sign.

'Shit, shit, shit,' I mutter, staring at the printer, willing the green light to reappear.

'The power's going to be out for a while.' The librarian is swiping his finger across his phone screen. 'Apparently, some lightning has struck something and taken out a transformer.'

'Blast! I was hoping to leave the petitions at a few places this afternoon and get some signatures.' I move closer to the librarian as he shows me the outage details on his phone screen.

'Leave it with me. Library's closing soon, but I'll wait around for a bit and, if the power comes back, I'll print some and see if I can grab some signatures this afternoon when I'm at the shops. Either way, I'll get some ready for tomorrow, and I'm happy to wander around the market before the jetty lighting to chat and spread the word.'

'Oh, that would be awesome. Thank you. My plate is full with the choir stuff and I wanted to make the most of all the families being in town tomorrow.'

'You'll get a lot of support. Families have been crying out for some type of care for years.'

'Yes, that's the vibe I'm getting, too, and my parents have promised to make some phone calls to the councillors and also to businesses about additional funding or investment.'

'Wow, that's great. I'll keep you posted.'

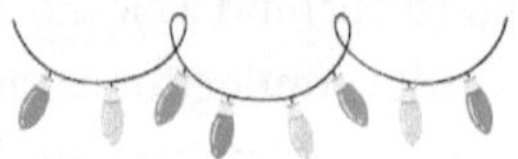

By the time I arrive at Seaside Village, I'm a sweaty mess. The back of my tee is damp, and wisps of hair are stuck to my forehead. The afternoon sea breeze hasn't yet arrived, and the sun burns when it comes out from behind the clouds.

Thankfully, the recreation hall is cool, due to the backup generator, and although the lights are off, there's a lot of natural light coming through the enormous windows that grant vast views of the bay.

On a makeshift stage, the choir members gather, their voices blending as they prepare for their performance. The staff has arranged the residents in a semicircle, sitting them in a mix of recliners and plastic chairs, their walkers, or their beds with the backrests raised. The room is full of tinsel and has handmade snowflakes hanging from the ceiling, with crepe-paper chains strung from one corner of the room to the other. It's all very festive, and I do an internal cheer and clap my hands like an excited six-year-old.

My heart breaks and melts simultaneously as the residents' faces transform into broad smiles as Greta enters the room dressed as a cheeky elf. There are claps and 'woohoos' as a bubble machine is turned on, and a couple of the choir members do an impromptu song and dance with the hand-held bells.

Marion—the village director—joins me inside the door. 'The residents have been so excited and are really looking forward to this. They don't get events like this where they can all gather for a singalong. We don't have enough staff or can't keep them long enough.'

'Gosh, that is so sad, Marion.' It wouldn't take much for this to be a regular event. I'm sure the choir members would enjoy getting together more than once a year, too. There are so many calendar events that can be celebrated with music—not just Christmas. 'Marion, would you be open to a chat about some ongoing music events like this?'

Her eyes widen. 'What are you suggesting? Aren't you heading back to Adelaide next week?'

'Well, that's the thing. I quit my job and have nothing to return to. And in the space of today, I've seen a need for both childcare and now something like this for the village residents. I'm in a position where I can offer both. If I can get the child-care up and running, it might mean your staffing issues would lessen.'

'Yes, it would. That's one of the main reasons they tell me they can't continue working or take on additional shifts. And

I hear there's a certain young nurse that might be playing a part in this decision, too?' A cheeky smirk crosses her face. 'According to Greta, that is.' Bless Greta (tongue in cheek) and her gossiping ways. I really wish she wouldn't do it or get involved in other people's business. Marion's smile is broad. 'I'd love to chat more with you about this. I've been thinking about putting on an entertainment-come-events-come-things-to-do person in the new year, even for just a day a week or as needed. Does that sound like something you'd be interested in?'

There's a lightness in my chest that hasn't been there in a long time. Since before all the shit with Stephanie and the centre went down.

'Oh wow, that would be amazing! I'm gathering signatures on a petition to present to the council to use the Hanna Charlton donation funds for a childcare centre to be built or a property purchased and converted, but in the meantime, I'm going to set up family day care to help as many families as I can. And I'd love to help out here, too.'

I pull Marion into a hug and whisper my thanks. A buzz of excitement zips around my chest, and goosebumps break out on my arms. There are so many possibilities. Ideas swoosh around my head. Suddenly, I have two jobs, a council fight on my hands and a relocation to organise.

'That would be absolutely fantastic.' Marion steps back. 'From what I've heard, there's been a lot of debate over the donation, and they've not come to any decision. I will one hundred percent back your petition and support you in any way possible. It's a much-needed service that never seems to be able to get up and running.'

When my phone vibrates in my shorts pocket, I slip it out, swiping to bring up the message on the screen. Those butter-flies in my stomach wake at the sight of his name, the memory of his kiss, the feel of his body ...

Ryan: Are you free to come over for dinner?

Me: Sure … just at Seaside Village and will come after.

Ryan: Great! I have some exciting news.

Me: Oh? Me too 😊

Ryan: Can't wait xx

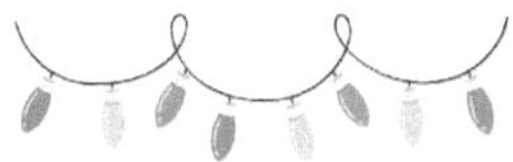

The concert at the village is a tremendous success with everyone joining in and singing along. Those who are able to, dance around the room and staff scoot other residents around on their wheels. There's twirling, line dancing, foot stomping and voracious clapping and hooting. The room is brought to tears when I sing 'Hallelujah', accompanied by Tom (who drops in with Carter and Woody for a visit) on the piano. And we finish with everyone singing 'Santa Claus is Coming to Town'.

Leaning against the wall, sipping a cold lemonade as I watch the residents bust out more dance moves like nobody's watching, my body is at odds with exhaustion and being on a sugar high. It's weighing heavily on me that I'm keeping something from Ryan. The truth is something I can no longer hide from him; it's time to come clean. The idea of revisiting Ryan's past hurts by sharing mine with him is daunting, but I've made up my mind to tell him tonight. My legs feel like they've trekked the coastal walk twice over, and there's a pinching ache between my shoulder blades … but I can't wait to do this again tomorrow night at the Lighting of the Jetty with water as the backdrop and a crowd of town locals singing along with their torches and battery-operated candles. It's going to be magical.

After playing a game of chess with resident Gordon while chatting about his life on the land and his excitement over seeing his grandkids tomorrow, I lend a hand to serve prawn cocktails for dinner in the dining room before saying my goodbyes.

Marion walks me out, and we plan to catch up soon. The new year is shaping up to be as bright as the jetty lights.

CHAPTER 13

Ryan

Grocery and gift shopping have been an adventure, to say the least. Purchasing the non-perishables for the food hampers for doing-it-tough families on Lilac's list is easy enough; I just grab all the things I wish I'd had on Christmas Day: pudding, custard, sugary cereal, chips and lollies. To the hampers, I add bags of pasta and rice, jars of pasta sauce and some tinned fruit and veggies. A bag of potatoes and some carrots will fill the boxes nicely.

But buying gifts for the kids is a challenge. Shopping in a small town means there isn't a lot to choose from, but I manage to grab enough from the supermarket, chemist, Marge's café and the newsagent.

With questioning stares from the locals, who must be wondering what's gotten into me and why I'm stocking up, I load everything into the back of the wagon and head home with a spring in my step. I'm going to be helping local families, and I have a date and news to share.

As I pull into the driveway, a large white shopping bag with a hint of something red peeking out from the top catches my attention on the front step. Really? Am I being pranked right now?

Sure enough, when I take a look-see inside the bag, I'm greeted by the sight of a perfectly folded Santa suit, ready to be worn. My jaw clenches. The high I'm on after my shopping expedition crashes down with the click of my fingers. There's a compelling urge to dump it in the wheelie bin and play innocent. It's one thing to spread joy behind the scenes quietly, but to dress up as Santa takes it to a whole new level, and it's one I'm not on board with. I rummage around in the bag for a note and find it pinned to the white beard:

Ryan, I've come down with what Marge has and don't want to spread it. Thought you'd make a great Santa ... You might just need some extra padding 😶 *Larry.*

'Why me? Surely there's someone else,' I mutter, pushing open the front door and dumping the bag in the spare room on the left. The rest of the gifts and hamper goodies can go in there too, out of the way. I'll deal with them tomorrow after my shift.

As I pull the bedroom door shut, there's a knock on the front screen door. Suddenly, I feel like a teenager again— sweaty palms, heart racing.

'Hey.' That seems to be all I can manage. My words have gone missing. I push the screen open and use my foot to wedge it there. Scarlett is holding the last of the shopping bags, including the one with the dinner food. And there's not a Christmassy thing anywhere on her body. Instead of her trademark festive tee, she's teamed her short shorts with a bright yellow tank, a delicate necklace and white Birks. She's skipped the Santa hat and gone for a casual look with a messy bun, and it's as sexy as all hell.

I reach out and stroke the back of my fingers down her cheek. 'Where's your glittery eyeshadow and Christmas attire?'

She takes my hand from her cheek and brings it to her lips,

kissing my palm, leaving a trace of strawberry lip gloss. Movement stirs in my crotch. Another kiss. 'I didn't want to dress up and continually shove the season in your face. I know it upsets you, and to be honest, there are other things to chat about tonight other than Christmas, right?'

'You did that for me?'

'I know I can be a bit over the top when it comes to anything festive; I want this Christmas to be better for you.'

With a gentle tug, I bring her into my arms, our bodies fitting perfectly together, as I bury my face in her neck, savouring the intoxicating blend of cinnamon and salt. 'You still smell like Christmas. Like those biscuits you were baking with your mum.'

'Hmmm.' Her fingers run through my hair, scratching my scalp.

'Get a room, you two!' A car rumbles past, and my eyes flick up to see Curly in his work ute.

'That was your brother. Shall we take this inside?' I ask.

'Let's.'

With the shopping bag in one hand and Scarlett's hand in the other, I lead her through the dark house and into the open-plan living area. The power is still out, but thankfully, the cool sea breeze has blown up, so I open the sliding doors leading onto the back deck.

'Nice digs.' Scarlett releases my hand and gazes around the mostly tidy area. Even though I haven't vacuumed for a while, I've folded and put away all my clothes and washed the dishes. She meanders through the room, past the suspended fireplace, her focus quickly shifting to the photos hanging on the wall. There are no family pictures whatsoever, but I have a keen eye for nature, and some of my favourite images are framed and displayed. 'I recognise some of these spots.' She points to one with a granite structure in front of a brilliant sunset. 'This is Murphy's Haystack.'

'It sure is.'

'And Turtle Rock near Wudinna. This one's Locks Well and'—she shuffles along the wall, pointing at the photos as she goes—'Winter Hill Lookout, and this last one is of the seals at Point Labatt.'

'I'm impressed you know your local tourist landmarks.'

'Well, I did grow up here, remember?'

'True, true.' I pull a paper-wrapped bundle from the shopping bag. 'Now, because the power is out, I thought we'd just do a cold dinner. You okay with salad and crayfish?'

'Um ... yes.' Scarlett laughs, returning to the kitchen, pulling out a stool and sliding onto it. 'Only if it's from Larry's boat.'

'You're in luck.'

Scarlett doesn't stay on the stool for long. As I deshell the crayfish, she gets out some plates, slices some lemon and chops tomatoes, cucumber and capsicum. We chat about nothing in particular but cover all the basics like previous jobs and relationships, travel destinations we've been to and want to visit, and our favourite AFL football teams ... I can't believe she's a Collingwood supporter. Of all the teams to follow. Her reasoning is that the Point Perry football and netball clubs feature black-and-white stripes with a magpie emblem. She is black and white, through and through, and nothing is going to change her, apparently.

I'm eager to share my news, but strangely, her mood tapers the further the evening progresses. She's gone unusually quiet as we relax on the lounges outside, enjoying a gin from Streaky Bay Distillers, and I can't contain myself any longer.

'Scarlett—'

'Ryan—'

We can't help but laugh, and I feel a mix of anticipation and awkwardness. Her cheeks flush and my heart flickers as I say, 'You go first.'

'Well.' She sips her drink. Why is she drawing this out? It must be news I don't want to hear. 'I have to go back to Adelaide—'

'No. I don't think you do.' My stomach drops, and I set the glass on the table. Grabbing her hands, I shake my head. She tries to pull away, but I won't budge. 'Please hear me out.'

'Ryan, there's something—'

'Today at the hall, you were in your element. You were amazing with the kids. I can see how much you love being with them, and that got me thinking.'

Scarlett is shaking her head, a slight smirk creeping across her face, but she's no longer trying to tug her hands away. Instead, she adjusts them so she's holding mine. 'Go on. What were you thinking?'

'Well, Hanna Charlton, the movie star from *Second Chance Love* who came home last year for the premiere, left a significant donation to the community—five hundred grand, I think; anyway, there's been no decision made as to what to do with it. So, when I ran into Mayor Hodgson, who showered me with thanks after looking after her son after a skateboarding accident, I tabled the idea of a childcare centre here in Point Perry. She was open and supportive of the idea, especially when I said … you might be willing to stay around and run it.' I slump back in the lounge. With a deep exhale, I reluctantly pull my hands away, and a wave of nervousness washes over me. 'But if you're going back to Adelaide …'

I can't read Scarlett's expression. It's impassive, and a frown burrows deeply between her brows. Her slight smile seems forced.

'What's going on? You don't like that idea?'

Scarlett scoots forward on the lounge until our knees touch. She clears her throat. 'I lied to you and told you everything was okay with the job I quit and the—' she swallows hard—'bullying. I know you've been hurt by liars in the past and bullies. I'm deeply sorry. I just want you to know everything before, well ... if this'—she waves her hand between us—'goes any further.'

I want 'this' to go further. I want her to say in Point Perry ... But lies, bullies?

'What happened? What has Stephanie done?' My voice is too sharp.

Her eyes become glassy with tears, and her fingers are twisting anxiously in her lap. 'It's a long story.' She takes a gulp of gin. 'Stephanie became jealous of the relationships I had with the parents and caregivers and the other employees. They all saw me as a leader, empathetic, easy to get along with, someone they could confide in. The more this happened, the more often Stephanie did things to me, to make me look bad, intimidate me, to the point where I had to take sick leave and get some help.'

I shake my head, not wanting it to be true that someone had hurt Scarlett. My emotions are in turmoil as I grapple with anger towards Stephanie, a deep sense of compassion for Scarlett, and a feeling of hurt stemming from her lack of trust in not sharing her situation with me when I explicitly asked. That she lied to me.

'Ryan, let me explain.'

When I hear the conviction in her voice, my heart wins out over any doubts or hesitation. Seeing her like this ... I suck in a breath. 'I'm listening.'

Scarlett swipes her tears away with the back of her hand.

'Stephanie is a larger-than-life, extrovert, attention-seeking, empathy-lacking person who believes the world owes her, and she will exploit anyone around her to get what she wants, no matter the impact. It soon became clear she lacked compassion and had no boundaries. She tells anyone and everyone about how successful she is, how influential she is, how she's the best in the industry ... a leader and innovator.

'Over time, this didn't sit right with me. Her narcissistic behaviour was at odds with my work ethics and values, and when I started to question her decisions and motives, she turned on me. She'd yell at me in front of staff and parents, assign tasks below my qualifications or that had nothing to do with the centre or give me so much work there was no way I could get it all done ... which she would then berate me for.

'Without warning, she would change my roster, and she would often embarrass me by discussing my personal life in front of and with colleagues during lunch breaks. All bullying and intimidating behaviours.

'Outside all of this, she stopped hiring casuals because it was too expensive and started lying to parents; we were over the required ratios, and she turned a blind eye, doing everything to cut costs. So many breaches. Every time I questioned her about them, she'd shoot me down, attack me with words or use my ideas and claim them as her own.

'I need to go back to Adelaide to see this through and make sure the truth is heard. I also have another appointment with my psychologist ... Stephanie really did a number on me. There are also more meetings with the department I need to attend.' She locks eyes with me, and determination flickers through them. 'But most importantly, now I've decided to stay in Point Perry, I needed you to know about this because I want everything to be out in the open for us.'

For us.

Relief hits me hard. She's staying? But there are questions. So many questions. A sea breeze whips across the deck, cooling my face. I shuffle on the lounge, lick my dry lips. What brings a tightening to my chest is the realisation she was being used, her joy in a job she loves slowly being stripped away, feeling trapped in a situation she'd endured for far too long.

'Why didn't you quit sooner? Why stay all that time?'

Her nose scrunches, and she rubs it with a serviette. 'The

kids and families are always my priority. I needed to be there to make sure they were still getting the best care, even though shit was happening behind the scenes. It took time to gather all the evidence. Only once the department was involved and the families were aware did I feel it was okay to leave.' She uses a serviette to wipe her tears and nose. 'She had the power over me, Ryan. For so long, I ignored the red flags because I wanted to see the good in her and what she was trying to do for the centre. I wanted her to be the genuine person she was making out to be. I didn't want to cause trouble. It was easier for me to go along with whatever she did as I hate conflict. But she eventually wore me down, and on top of the breaches, it all turned so toxic that I couldn't stay for the sake of my health and wellbeing.'

Taking her hands gently into my own, I press my lips against her knuckles. 'What a warrior you are for putting the clients ahead of yourself. For enduring it all this time. But also for recognising when it was too much and for seeking help. And thank you for opening up and telling me. Stephanie sounds like a real piece of work, and I hope she gets what she deserves.'

'So do I.' Scarlett briefly closes her eyes and sighs. 'The investigation will highlight her behaviour, workplace relationships and business decisions. It's up to the department to make a ruling and do what they need to do. But you are the one person I want to know the truth. I need you to understand the situation, the challenges I'm facing and the urgency for me to go back to the city.'

'I do, Scarlett. I'm sorry you had to experience that.'

'There is absolutely no need for you to apologise, as you have done nothing wrong. I just appreciate you giving me the time to explain and for listening.'

'Always.'

Our hands unravel, and her fingertips brush against my

bare thighs. A wave of warmth radiates up my leg. Awakens me. I try to move inconspicuously to hide my growing erection. All it takes is her touch now, and I'm a goner. Not even her work drama can dampen my admiration, my need to be close to her.

'You kind of said before you were staying in Point Perry. So you've made that decision. What changed since I saw you earlier?'

'As I was trying to say'—there's that beautiful smile again —'I have to go back to Adelaide'—she holds up her finger to stop me from butting in again—'not only to deal with the work stuff but to pack up my things. I want to make Point Perry my home.'

All the breath I've been holding suddenly rushes out. A flood of hope courses through me, pooling in my heart. 'Oh, thank God.' Inching closer, aiming for her lips, I'm halted by her raised hand. What now? My heart can't take any more.

'*I* also had the brilliant idea of using the donation to build a childcare centre. With Mum's help this afternoon, my idea is gaining traction with the locals who might invest the remaining money. I can sell my unit in the city, too, if need be. The town will part-own the business with me—a community partnership. I'm willing to risk my own home to make this work, and I presented a rough business proposal to Councillor Giles.' When her smile turns into a frown, my heart sinks. 'Which he dismissed straight away, saying none of the sitting councillors would be on side with the idea. However, I can't blame him, as I lobbed into his office when he was about to go on his holidays, and I showed him the proposal I had written in pencil in my notebook.

'So, I'm going to do a proper proposal and business plan, get all my facts and figures, and tomorrow at the market and jetty lighting, I'm going to get as many signatures as possible on a petition. Get around and talk to as many families and councillors as I can. I tried to get it started today, but the power went out just as I was about to print them.'

'But it could take a few years to build a centre, if it even gets approval. Or are you thinking of finding an established property and converting it? We can have a chat with Sebastian Conway—the local real estate agent. He might know of something available or coming available soon.'

The sparkle in her eyes returns, and she shuffles closer still. 'We?'

As I gently rest my hands on her arms, a surge of anticipation fills my stomach. I'm buzzing with the endless possibilities. The future. Could it be with Scarlett?

'Is it not clear I will do anything to keep you here? And if that means helping you get a childcare centre up and running, then I'm all in. If it means road tripping to Adelaide to sort out Stephanie, then I'm in the car with you. If it means holding you tight while you process your mental load, then I'm here with arms waiting to comfort you.'

The moment I finish speaking, her lips smack against mine. It's not passionate or full of heat; instead, it's a grateful, thank-you-for-being-on-my-side kiss. When she pulls back, she continues. 'In the meantime, I'll set up family day care. It'll be a start at helping some parents in need. I'll need to find somewhere to do that, too. I also need to get some public liability insurance and ...'

Finally, she stops for a breath, but just as I'm about to speak, she starts up again. 'And then this afternoon, when the choir was at Seaside Village, Marion asked if I'd be interested in working at the village on an entertainment program, likely one day a week or as needed. And I said yes!'

This time, when she stops talking, she fists her hands in the air and squeals with excitement. She is so bloody adorable and sexy. Her cheeks are flushed as she throws her arms around me.

'And while you're celebrating, I have more news for you.' I can't help but grin as she chews her bottom lip and sits on her hands. 'And you don't have to say yes or do it, and you might be too busy now with all your jobs, but ... Lilac needs a helper. They want to move her into Seaside Village for a time until she recovers as she lives by herself, but she is dead-set against the idea. She can stay in hospital for another day or so, but then she needs to go into the village or see if she can stay with someone until after Christmas as she's got no family. Is that something you might be keen on?'

Tears well in Scarlett's eyes. She points to them. 'These are happy tears, and yes! That would work perfectly.'

'She will be thrilled. She's such an independent soul, and we can work around all the other things you need to do. I'm sure others in the community can step in and help out, too.'

She lets out an enormous sigh and wipes her tears away. 'My gosh, I can't believe how everything has turned around in the space of today. I'm staying in Point Perry. Woohoo!'

My hands gently cradle her cheeks as our lips collide. This time, it's urgent, hungry, our tongues dancing. She crawls forward and straddles my lap, and I groan as our hips crash together. The heat's there, grinding and ... something digging into my back ... the lounge arm.

In one swift move, I stand. Scarlett wraps her legs around my waist, and I stride through the kitchen, where I grab the box of condoms from the shopping bag.

'Presumptuous much?' Scarlett's breath is hot on my neck. 'You know buying those from the IGA is only going to fuel the rumour mill.'

'I'll be happy to tell the world I'm with you.'

CHAPTER 14

Scarlett

Ryan's scratchy beard tickles across my shoulders, rousing me from a deep, blissful sleep. I stretch my arms above my head, arching my back, my body deliciously sore from last night.

'What time is it?' A yawn escapes, and I cover my mouth with my hand to smother it. Rolling over, I come face-to-face with a sexy, sleepy face. 'Good morning.'

'It's early.' He plants a kiss on my nose.

It's the sweetest thing. His aftershave of sandalwood and musk and the washing detergent from his fresh scrubs tickle my nose. It's heady and fast becoming my favourite smell—even better than Mum's Christmas pudding or honey biscuits. There's nothing I want more than to bring him on top of me and resume what we were doing last night.

'I start at seven for day shift.' His grumbly, gravelly morning voice does nothing to quell the need.

'Urgh.' There goes that plan.

'Go back to sleep. I'll catch you later.'

'Later, as in for the Lighting of the Jetty?' There's been a shift from his grinchiness over the last day or so, which seems relatively quick, and I'm yet to work out why. I really hope he can put some of his past anxieties and bad experiences behind him and see how the community rallies around.

'Possibly.' He nuzzles my neck, sending a pulse straight to my core. 'I have a couple of errands to run after my shift.'

'Hmmm, okay. Come find me. I'll be around the markets with my petition or with the choir or eating Conway's butterscotch ice cream, hot doughnuts or barbeque sausages.'

Before I can roll over and go back to sleep, his lips are pressed to mine, searing and quick, enough to leave me breathless and tingling down below.

'Gotta go or I'll be late.' He presses his forehead against mine. 'Thank you.'

'For what?'

'For making me see a different side to Christmas. For making me realise there's more to it than my shitty childhood. That it's time to leave the past in the past. That I can make a difference.' He peppers kisses down my nose. 'And it's all because of you.'

My heart constricts so intensely, like it's trapped in a vice. 'It's all you, Ryan. All I did was shove my Christmas cheer in your face and accuse you of the petty crime of not being my pen pal when we were seventeen.'

'No, you showed me there's more to Christmas than a family who doesn't make it special. You made me open my eyes and look around at how others celebrate, how the community celebrates ... how it's bigger than me.'

There's such an earnest look in his eyes. A look of rediscovery, anticipation. Of possibility.

'Ryan, this might be a bit forward, but I hope we have more Christmases together and—'

'I do too.' His entire face lights up like a twinkling star on top of the tree. 'But if I don't go, I might be the one out of a job.'

'Okay.' I give him a gentle push against his chest, and he reluctantly climbs off. 'Catch you later.'

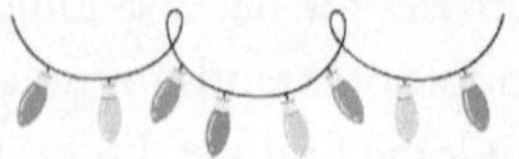

By three in the afternoon, even though I can't wipe the smile off my face, and I have a spring in my step, I'm ready for a nanna nap. From my Christmas Eve to-do list, I've ticked off: choir at the supermarket, discussion with two councillors, emailing Hanna Charlton, erecting marquees in the foreshore car park for the markets, clean the footy club barbeque and taste test the Lions Club hot doughnuts. I've also dropped in on Lilac at the hospital, shared the good news and put a plan in place to get her home ASAP. Over a cuppa, she told me about a TV show she was watching called *Old People's Home for 4 Year Olds* and jokingly said we should set that up at her house with the family day care kids. The idea isn't as silly as it sounds.

The library guy dropped off a clipboard with the petition sheets at the IGA when we were singing, and everyone I spoke with, passed in the street or came within twenty metres of were willing listeners and most signed. Some offered to discuss my plan with the councillors, too, which could be a huge help.

Thankfully, the weather gods are looking upon the town, and the hot, windy, dry, stormy weather has blown away, replaced with blue skies and a lovely salty sea breeze.

The market is alive with activity as the vendors hang festive-coloured bunting and meticulously arrange their tables, showcasing an assortment of homemade crafts, freshly baked treats, fragrant candles, delicate jewellery and crafted wood-work. The lovely folk from Streaky Bay Distillers are setting up a gin and vodka tasting stand, and there are fresh crayfish and prawns available, too—the crayfish reminding me of last night, of Ryan and his arms wrapped tightly around me.

A grassed area under the trees has been layered with picnic rugs for the children to gather on when Santa arrives, who is usually Larry. But I've heard on the grapevine that he and Marge are laid up with the flu and that someone else has been organised. So long as the kids are looked after, that's all that counts.

As the town converges on the foreshore car park, the PA system plays Christmas hits from Wham! and Mariah Carey. Dad and a couple of the other locals string the last of the fairy lights between the light poles on the jetty. That tingling, exciting, magical feeling radiates through my body. Families find spaces on the lawn to spread their picnic rugs out, laughing children dance around and watch the sky for Santa, and tins from local breweries and food for platters come out of an assortment of Eskys and food coolers.

At the far end of the car park, away from the market stalls and festivities, there's a small group of people gathered around a vehicle. A couple hug and shake hands with a guy before walking away with a cardboard box in each hand. Then another couple, and another, until the group separates, and next to his station wagon stands Ryan, handing over a fishing rod and tackle box to a man with a small boy.

Ryan's bought food and gifts for those families doing it tough. That must've been what he was doing yesterday when he said he had some things to do.

Witnessing the tender moment when the boy hugs Ryan, my emotions overwhelm me, causing tears to well up and slowly make their way down my face. A solid lump forms in my throat, and I curse myself for not having a bottle of water with me.

I make my way over to Ryan as the last people leave, but he jumps into his car and heads up the hill towards the main street. I get him leaving, not wanting to be in the jubilant, festive crowd and getting attention from everyone. The good-souled man just wanted to help outside the prying eyes of a gossipy community, and I understand that.

As I swipe at my eyes, my feet remain rooted to the asphalt, and I contemplate the selfless, random act of kindness Ryan just delivered. This man who hates Christmas has a heart of gold.

I let out a deep sigh as my name is called over the PA system. Time to rally the choir.

The one thing I definitely didn't expect is getting a standing ovation. But if I'm being perfectly honest, we did sound pretty good. The harmonies were on point, and the deep baritones by Graham were the best I've heard him sing.

The crowd chants, 'More, more, more.'

As I glance towards the side of the stage, I notice Lilac there with Nurse Barb. Together, we guide her to a chair on the stage, where she takes hold of a microphone and leads the choir in a rousing performance of 'We Wish You a Merry Christmas'.

When we finish, I suck in some deep breaths to calm my breathing and quickly scan the running sheet before clicking the microphone back into its stand.

'Thank you, everyone.' The crowd roars again, lifting their drinks and tinsel-adorned wands. There's a real buzz amongst the crowd that's spread across the sand and lawned areas. Kids holding glow sticks aloft are dodging people sitting in deck chairs. 'Please keep that cheer going for the amazing Point Perry Choir and its fearless leader … Aunt Lilac.' I step aside and gesture to the group who are grinning with their arms around each other.

I step up to the microphone again. The crowd settles, and a hush falls over the gathering. 'I also want to take this opportunity to thank everyone who's signed the petition to support a childcare centre here in Point Perry.'

Applause runs through the crowd. There are even wolf whistles, and someone yells, 'About bloody time.'

'I'll be continuing discussions with Mayor Hodgson and Councillor Giles in the new year. If you feel strongly about this cause, I'd encourage you to speak with the sitting councillors and share your thoughts about how it will benefit the community. In the interim, I'll be setting up some much-needed day care options once I get sorted.'

The crowd shouts cheers of 'thank you' and 'can't wait'.

'Now, I have it on good authority that a certain special someone is on his way, so can all the children gather under the tree where the big red chair is.'

A massive commotion ensues as children, large and small, sprint, skip and dawdle to where a large, wooden gingerbread house has been erected behind a big red chair. Local photographer Beccy has her tripod set up and is ready to capture the sweet—or not-so-sweet—moments between the children and Santa.

As I search the bustling crowd, my eyes darting from face to face, Ryan is nowhere to be seen. Some small part of me thought ... hoped he might've returned to join the festivities or at least watch the choir.

Out on the water, the distinct hum of a motor becomes louder, signalling the approach of something or someone. Instead of sitting and waiting, the children eagerly sprint towards the water's edge as a Santa-clad Jet Ski rider zooms towards the beach.

'Ho, ho, ho.' Santa pulls the ski to a stop on the shoreline and cuts the engine. 'Who wants some presents?'

Santa readjusts his stomach padding and reaches behind the seat to pull out a large sack. As he does so, his white beard slips, revealing a dark beard underneath. That familiar dark beard left a rash on my breast last night; was between my legs in the early hours of this morning.

When our eyes finally meet across the tops of the children's heads, there's no doubt they're Ryan's ocean-blue eyes, and there's a happy sparkle glittering in them. A million unsaid words transpire between us. My heart skips a beat, and I have to rest my hand over my chest to calm the frantic pounding. As much as I want to push the kids aside and take Santa all for myself, pull him into my arms and tell him how proud of him I am and how brave he is, I can't. This is about the children, and I have to wait my turn.

'Okay, kids, go sit down and let me get through.' Santa hoists the bag over his shoulder and makes towards the big red chair.

There's a tug on my arm. 'Hello, Evie.' My niece stares at me, bottom lip quivering. 'What's the matter?'

'Aunty Lettie, I can't find Mummy or Daddy and Santa scares me a little bit. Can you come with me? Can I sit with you?' Her eyes are wide, and the usually cheeky girl slinks back behind my legs, supposedly out of sight from Santa.

Santa Ryan crouches down—bare feet and all—at eye level with Evie. 'Hello, what's your name?'

'It's Evie.' She risks a peek around my leg, and I gently rest my hand on her shoulder.

'Ah, Evie. I saw on my list that you've been very good this year. You tried really hard at school and are a good friend.'

Evie nods against my leg and cautiously steps forward.

'And'—Santa Ryan rummages around in his sack—'yes,

here it is. A gift for you.' He hands the small red box over, and Evie hesitantly takes it.

'Thank you,' she whispers. 'I'll leave a cookie out for you and a carrot for your reindeer.'

'Oh, Evie, how very kind of you. I look forward to it, and my reindeer are always hungry. Thank you.'

There's a hesitant shake of hands. When Ryan stands, we're almost face-to-face; his rounded stomach is lumpy and lopsided, and then he winks. Winks!

'You're very kind, Santa.' I can't help but smile. 'And now you'd better hand out the other gifts before there's a riot.'

Forty-five minutes later, the last present is gifted, and there's a mountain of wrapping paper under the shelter, ready for recycling. Children run around enjoying the ten-dollar-maximum gifts their parents provided for the celebration, and adults feast on grilled whiting sandwiches, barbeque meat or prepacked picnic hampers.

The day isn't over yet; the sun is still hovering well above the horizon, and thanks to daylight savings, it won't be setting for a while.

It's still a while before the official Lighting of the Jetty—time enough for The Longest Cast competition. The jetty is filling with entrants and their fishing lines and this year, Dad is the judge. Let's hope it doesn't end with a big, tangled mess.

Lilac—having gotten a leave pass from hospital—is settled on a camp chair with some of the choir members and Greta has offered to make sure she's okay, fed, watered, socialised and to return her to the hospital when she's ready.

Santa Ryan squats in front of her, much like he did with Evie, and they chat quietly, intently. Lilac breaks into a wide smile before planting a kiss on his cheek.

I lip read, and she says, 'I'm proud of you.'

Ryan squeezes her good hand and works his way around the crowd, wishing people Merry Christmas and shaking hands with farmers and townsfolk before finally arriving where I stand next to the Jet Ski to make sure none of the kids take off on it.

'Well, Santa, you are full of surprises.' There's no way I can hide the big grin on my face.

'I have one more.' He leans in, his furry beard tickling my cheek. 'I know a great place to watch the lights. You interested?'

I pull back and study his face. Desperate to remove the costume and see the 'normal' Ryan, to read his face properly, to run my hands through his hair, I nod. 'Sure, and if it means I get to sit behind Santa on a Jet Ski, I'm all for it.'

'Your chariot awaits.' He settles on the seat and attaches the safety cord around his wrist while I grab a lifejacket from Curly's boat anchored next to the ski. 'You need a jacket?'

'Nah.' He pats his stomach. 'It's under my suit.'

I chuckle and splash through the shallow water, climb on the ski and settle behind him. My arms slip around his padded waist. As the engine starts, a couple of the bigger kids push us out from the shoreline and the remainder of the crowd waves, hoots and hollers. My cheeks hurt from grinning.

With my chin resting on his shoulder and the sea salt splashing my face, I press my lips to his ear. 'I'm so proud of you, Ryan Black.'

CHAPTER 15

Ryan

Heading from the crowded beach around the cove and away from view, I direct the ski towards the boat ramp, desperate to get out of this costume, which is itchy and hot as hell. After all the apprehension, anxiety and dread at playing the part of a man I never really knew growing up, the smiles of the kids made it worth it. The parents and community, the happiness, the anticipation, the eagerness, and the act of giving have all filled my heart with light and gratitude. It's changed my view on the true meaning of Christmas and the concept of family beyond blood ties. And the possibilities of what letting your walls down and challenging your beliefs can lead to.

I'm so proud of myself, too, for the memories that have plagued me for all these years will no longer have a hold over me. The power my 'parents' had has been squashed. But most importantly, I've got the girl. One who's staying in Point Perry. One who wants to spend more Christmases with me. One who's—

'Ryan! Look out!'

Crunch.

Scarlett's hands loosen from my waist. Where there was heat between our bodies, there's now coolness.

Weightlessness.

A scream. A splash.

Cold. My eyes sting when I open them under the water. Saltwater fills my mouth.

Silence.

As my lifejacket tugs me upwards, I emerge from the water and am met with panicked screams. But not Scarlett's.

The Jet Ski floats unmanned nearby. The shore's about fifty metres away.

With frantic movements, I thrash about, fighting to free myself from the Santa pants and yank the coat off my arms, all the while keeping a sharp lookout for Scarlett.

There's no sign of her anywhere. Shit. She must be under the water, but she had her life jacket on. I should be able to see her. Where is she?

The rapid thumping of my heart vibrates through my entire body.

'Scarlett?' I cough, blinking rapidly into the setting sun.

Next to the ski, a small tinny floats upside down, motor off.

With a massive kick, I surge through the water, ploughing my arms through the surface. Where is she? Where is she?

'Help!' Not Scarlett's voice.

'Scarlett? Where are you?' Why can't I see her? Fuck. Searching, my eyes scan the top of the ocean. Still nothing.

I unclick and remove my life jacket, suck in a deep breath and duck dive towards the ocean floor, opening my eyes, twisting around, searching in every direction. Legs thrash around near the edge of the boat.

As I emerged to the surface, I spot two figures clinging to the edge of the small boat near the stationary motor. They're just kids, young boys, barely in their early teens.

'Where are your life jackets? Who else was on the boat with you?' I pass my life jacket to the younger of the boys, and he hugs it tight. 'Where's Scarlett? The lady on the back of my ski? Have you seen her?'

'Sorry. Just us two. Didn't mean ... the sun. Couldn't see ... you,' the older boy blubbers as he helps the younger one grip the boat.

Under the boat ... She must be ... Shit.

I suck in a deep breath and push under. And there she is, on her stomach, head submerged, hair floating out in a fan. My lungs burn as I hold my breath for longer. I manoeuvre around her, grab the shoulders of her life jacket and kick and pull simultaneously. She doesn't budge. I let go and feel around her body, trying to pull her from whatever she's stuck on. Her life jacket is caught on something.

There's a claustrophobic tightening in my lungs. I need air.

I pop up in an air pocket between the seats and heave in a breath, gasp for another one, refill them.

I push back under Scarlett. My fingers fumble with the plastic clips as I desperately try to unclick the secure lifejacket. Eventually, all three come undone. Her arms slip free, and she slowly drifts downwards, causing me to tightly grip her armpits and propel us away from the boat with a single, powerful flutter kick.

Surging upwards, I break the surface and hastily gulp in a lungful of air. 'Scarlett, can you hear me? C'mon, breathe.'

Gently, I flip her onto her back and press my fingers into her carotid artery. There's a pulse—a faint one. A gash on the back of her head is spewing blood. Shit. I tread water, manoeuvring around her so I can support her head and neck. There's no breath, no rising and falling of her chest.

My legs are burning, my lungs are burning, but I keep kicking, churning them to stay afloat.

I pinch her nose, press my lips over hers and breathe into her lungs.

'C'mon, Scarlett. Breathe. Damn it.'

Nothing.

When I check her eyes, they appear glassy. Her pulse is still thready. The longer she goes without breathing, the worse it will be.

The shore. Get to the shore.

'Boys, can you swim to the shore? Come with me.'

The older one emerges from the opposite side of the boat, pulling along the younger one, who thankfully still holds onto the jacket.

'You'll be right. Stay close to me. It's not far. You're doing a great job.' My legs are on autopilot, kicking furiously as I pull Scarlett to the shore. 'C'mon, Scarlett. I can't lose you. I'm sorry I didn't see them. It's all my fault.'

I huff another breath into her lungs.

Her lips are blue. I recheck her pulse. Still thready, but there.

'Stay with me, Scarlett. Not long now.' Her nonresponse sends my heart and head spiralling. I've done this to her. 'I'm sorry,' I whisper into her ear. God, if she doesn't survive or has brain damage from not enough oxygen ... and her Christmas will be ruined; it means so much to her.

I'm a Christmas curse. Always have been, always will be.

Nothing good has ever come from this shitty time, ever. This should be me not breathing. I don't deserve to be on this earth.

I heave another breath into her lungs.

My body is stiff, cramping, and apart from the pounding in my head and the blood sloshing through my heart, nothing else seems to be working. As I'm hauling Scarlett along beside me, a wave ripple forms and splashes into my mouth.

Yelling. People are yelling from the shore. And splashing.

The boys are okay, still near me. I won't take my eyes from Scarlett to see, though. I hope Deb and Bronte are there with the ambulance.

My feet finally touch sand, and I dig my toes into the ocean floor to gain some traction, and I continue to haul Scarlett to safety.

'Ryan? You with us, mate?' someone calls. 'Here. Grab my arm and let go of Scarlett. Tom and Curly are here and will get her onto the sand.'

'No. I ... need ... need breathe for Scarlett. CPR.'

'It's okay, mate. Ambos are here.'

I nod, give in, latch onto Fabian. 'Give her ... breath. Please don't ... let her ...'

Moments later, Fabian drags me onto the shore, and a commotion ensues in a blur. Jack ploughs into the water and, with Tom's help, loops his hands under her shoulders and knees, taking her out of the water and onto the sand.

Rae runs to Scarlett's side and drops to her knees, clutching her daughter's limp hand.

Deb kneels at Scarlett's head, placing the bag and mask over her mouth and nose, pushing a breath into her lungs. Bronte's by her side, starting chest compressions.

Deb is reeling off questions: Who can tell me what happened? How long was she under the boat for? How fast were they travelling? Where's Ryan?

'I'm here.' I hover, feeling useless. Too many people crowd Scarlett. Answer the questions. Someone wraps a towel around my shoulders. It's happening in slow motion. Wish I could rewind the clock. It's like I'm floating above, watching, unable to move.

Councillor Giles is clearing the gathering crowd, pushing them back. Sarge has taken the two boys aside, and they're sitting morosely with their parents next to the police wagon, towels wrapped around their bodies.

It's not long before they load Scarlett into the ambulance and, with the doors closed, they track across the sand and head to the hospital. I sway slightly and squeeze my eyes shut, unable to look at the retreating vehicle, knowing this whole situation is my doing, my fault.

'Do you want a lift? You probably need to be checked out too?' Tom steadies me with a hand on my shoulder and offers me a bottle of cold water, which I eagerly drink.

'Nah, I'm okay. My wagon is here in the car park. I'll just catch my breath and then head up to the hospital. Thanks again for your help.'

'No worries, mate. You did a great thing in saving her.'

More like nearly killing her. That's not the man I want to be. Not the man Scarlett wants to be with.

All I want to do now is go back into the ocean, sink to the bottom and be carried away by the tide.

CHAPTER 16

Scarlett

Beep, beep, swoosh.

Shuffling noises. Murmurs, male and female. The smell of disinfectant wafts past my nose. Bright light pierces my eyes as I struggle to open them. I shiver.

Flashes of silver, of being on the Jet Ski ... the water. Not being able to breathe. Of ...

'Where's Ryan?' My voice is harsh, croaky and shaking. It feels like sandpaper has been rubbed along the length of my throat, leaving it raw. A dull thud holds court at the back of my head, and I turn it to the side for relief. 'He hurt too?' The words are hard to form.

I remember being on the Jet Ski, holding him tight, proud, happy then ... silver ...

Nurse Barb holds a plastic cup with a straw in it to my lips. 'Take a little sip. It'll help your throat.'

She presses buttons on the beeping machine next to my bed as Doctor Cruikshank writes something in a white folder, brows furrowed.

'There we go.' Barb places the cup back on the bedside table.

'Ryan?' Frustrated, I try again, this time putting more conviction into my voice. Why is no one answering my question?

Barb and Doctor Cruickshank exchange a look I can't quite decipher.

My heart thunders behind my aching ribs. I don't want to ask, but I need to know. They can't keep it from me. I need the truth. We were on the ski together and now ...

'Is he—? Oh, God, no. Please ...' My breath catches; my chest squeezes like I'm drowning all over again. I try to suck in air. Can't. Hurts. Is this a bad dream?

Barb's warm hand rests on my arm, tender where a cannula has been inserted. 'He's okay, love. He wasn't injured. He saved you.'

Saved me? A cry of relief bursts from my parched, cracked lips. Ryan's alive, and he saved me. Tears well, and I swipe at them with my thumb. Barb hands me a box of tissues, and I pull a few out and blow my nose. There's still a disarming look in her eyes, though.

'What, Barb? Is there something else? What happened? If he's okay ... saved me. I thought he'd be here.'

'Love, now don't be alarmed; everything is under control—'

'But ...'

'We're not sure where he is.'

I jerk fully upright on the hospital bed, trying to make sense of what Barb's saying. The machine beeps frantically. 'What do you mean? I don't understand.'

'Take a deep breath, Scarlett. Your heart has had a bit of a rough time today, and we need to look after it.'

'But Ryan is missing? You have to find him. Make sure he's okay. Christmas isn't a great time for him. Please—' My fingers tingle, and I slump back on the raised bedhead, totally sapped of energy. Need to fight, find Ryan, but so damn tired.

It's all my fault. Those four words ring in my ears. Oh no. No, no, no.

'I need to speak with him. Call him. He thinks this is all his fault.'

'You need to take it easy, Scarlett.' Doctor Cruikshank rests his hand on my shoulder. 'Your body had been through a massive trauma. It needs to recover and heal, and placing undue stress on it isn't helping. I can give you a sedative if you'd like.'

'Undue stress! And no.' I tighten my jaw. Swallow. Lick my dry lips. 'The guy who saved me, who is dealing with his trauma, whom I care deeply about, who blames himself, needs me right now. And unless you're willing to discharge me, I suggest you get me a phone so I can damn well call him.' I suck in one breath and another.

I lock eyes with the doctor, and a silent argument passes between us; neither of us breaks our stare until Barb hands me her mobile, Ryan's number on the screen, ready to call.

I take the phone and, with shaky hands, tap the call button. It rings and rings. Eventually, his voicemail picks up. Hearing his voice sends a sliver of relief through me. Just the sound, the sweet sound, is enough to cause my heart to speed up again.

'Ryan, honey, it's me ... Scarlett. Just borrowing Barb's phone. Where are you? I'm okay. Come back to the hospital, please. I need to see you. Or ring. I know this is a really tough time for you.' I bite my bottom lip to halt the tears. 'Please. It was just a freak accident. I need you. It's not your fault. None of this is your fault.' *Nothing in your childhood is your fault.*

The sob escapes, and I try to cover it with a cough. As the voicemail beeps to signal its conclusion, I hand the phone back to Barb.

Exhaustion washes over me; a yawn stretches the dried cracks of my lips. My eyelids droop. But I need to find Ryan.

'Barb, help me find him.' I muster all my energy and sit up, swinging my legs over the side of the bed. Determination courses through me, almost giving me a second wind. 'I want to discharge myself.'

'No, Scarlett.' Barb exchanges a concerned look with the doctor. 'You were very close to being flown out to the hospital in Adelaide, and there is a risk of secondary drowning. You need to stay here and be monitored.'

As my feet touch the floor, I lock eyes with Barb, my gaze unwavering. 'I need to go, and I will ... with or without you. And I promise I will come straight back when he's found.'

Barb hesitates, pressing her lips together before shaking her head. 'People are out looking for him. I'll get an update for you. He can't have gone too far.'

'How do you know that? He could be anywhere. Please, Barb.' I stand and gently tug on the IV line, wincing as the needle moves in the back of my hand.

Barb's hand is on mine in an instant. 'Here, let me.' She pulls on a fresh pair of gloves, turns off the drip machine and gently removes the line. 'Why are you so determined?'

'The lights. We were going to watch the lights turn on ... together.'

CHAPTER 17

Ryan

I don't make it to the hospital.

I'd reassured everyone I was okay and said I would follow the ambulance, but when I climbed into my wagon and drove from the car park, I couldn't. I couldn't watch the woman I was falling in love with be taken away, in that situation, when it was all my fault. When she wouldn't have almost drowned if it weren't for my inattention. I should've stayed away altogether, away from the festivities, the joy, like I did every other year.

All I want is to be where no one will find me. I don't want to go home, but I can't bring myself to leave town. That feels too final, and I promised Lilac I would do a few odd jobs to make her coming home easier. So when I come to the crossroad in the middle of town, I turn away from the hospital and end up in Lilac's house.

After securing the safety grip handle next to the toilet, I slide down Lilac's bathroom wall and place the electric drill on the floor tiles. Time has slipped away unnoticed.

Bowing my head and closing my eyes, I struggle to keep the images of Deb and Bronte working on Scarlett at bay. The chest compressions, checking her vitals, the moment she coughed up seawater … the moment I knew she'd be okay, alive …

There's so much noise pressing in on me: people yelling, children screaming, boat motors rumbling, Christmas carols, waves crashing, someone calling my name.

Voices are in my head. Scarlett's mother screaming it's all my fault. Curly calling me the 'Christmas Curse'. My father bellowing that I've been naughty so there will be no presents.

A curse. From the day I was born, I've been a Christmas curse. Unwanted. Unloved. Unworthy.

And just when I thought I'd put an end to the curse, it's come back with a vengeance, causing harm to the one who's allowed me love. Made me believe something else was possible.

The wall in front of me morphs into the back of the floral lounge I hid behind as a kid. The voices are too loud. Screaming over each other. Screeching in unison. My breaths are rugged, short, sucking, shallow. Eyes squeeze shut. Heart threatens to crash through my ribs. Pins and needles, hands, feet, tingling. I cover my ears with my hands. Squeezing them tight.

'No! Don't yell at me. Don't hit me.' I thrash my head to the side, twisting into the corner of the bathroom. 'Don't … sorry.'

'Ryan.' Warm hands rest over mine. I try to flick them away, press my palms harder to block the noise. Then they're back, slowly gliding my hands down my cheeks. 'Ryan, honey, you're safe. No one's going to hurt you.'

That voice. Familiar. Angel. Can't breathe.

'Ryan, you're okay. You're safe. Can you take a big breath in through your nose? Into your tummy.'

Those warm hands are gently squeezing mine now, and for a moment, the haze clears, the breathing's easier.

'That's right. And again. Let it all out through your

mouth. No one's here to hurt you; no one's yelling. Nothing is your fault.'

With each breath, the buzzing in my chest lessens, and the tingling in my fingers and toes all but recedes. When I dare to open my eyes, it's Scarlett that comes into focus. Her eyes are clear, bright, full of worry. Nothing like they were in the ocean. Even wearing oversized scrubs, with a cannula stuck in place, and sandy, straggly hair, she is beautiful. And I nearly lost her. My inattention almost caused great heartache for so many.

'Scar ... Scarlett. You ... hospital? What are you doing here? You don't want to be around me. I'm cursed. It's Christmas, and ... accident. I'm sorry. I wasn't concentrating. Should ...'

Scarlett rests her forefinger on my lips. 'Shhh.' She winces as she manoeuvres her body to sit between my legs. When I hold my hands out to stop her, push her away, she shakes her head. 'Na-up. No more of this pushing me away.'

When she gasps in pain and presses her hand to her chest, instinctively, I reach out and place my hand on hers, around hers, holding them tight. The pain in her ribs must be excruciating. God, I'm a shitty person to do this to her. I don't deserve her.

'Don't you dare think it's your fault.'

'But—' How can she think this?

'No! I can read your mind a mile away. That's why you didn't come to the hospital, why you're hiding away here. Ryan, you saved me. *You* saved me from a freak accident that no one knew would happen. *You* kept me alive, breathing for me when I couldn't, giving me a chance until I got to shore.'

I bow my head and shake it, unable to bear the kindness, the compassion reflected in her eyes. 'You've got it all wrong. If I didn't ask you to sit on the back of the Jet Ski, none of this would've happened. I tried too hard to change and look where it left me—back at square one. Ruining everyone's Christmas.'

With a gentle touch, Scarlett raises my chin, and our eyes instantly connect. Something warm unfurls in my stomach. There's no pity or sympathy in her eyes. Instead, there's empathy. Kindness. Understanding.

'No one's Christmas has been ruined, Ryan. It's quite the opposite. The families you provided hampers for will have a special meal to treasure. Those kids you bought gifts for will have the best day ever. And you brought so much joy and happiness to so many people in our community this afternoon. The smiles on the kids' faces … you did that, Ryan.' She pulls my head closer, grimacing. 'I'm so darn proud of you.'

With her lips gently touching my forehead, my eyes automatically shut, and I let out a sigh of relief.

'And I'm going to be okay. Even though Barb and Doctor Cruickshank are less than impressed I'm here.'

'How did you know where to find me?'

'Greta. As I was trying to negotiate my release, she was returning Lilac to the hospital and mentioned, among other things, that she saw you in the hardware store earlier in the day buying some rails. And after our discussion about getting Lilac back home, I just knew you'd be here. Barb reluctantly agreed to let me come, but only if she could be the one driving. She's waiting in the car to take me back to the hospital.'

Tenderly, I clasp her face in my hands and gently press my lips against hers. 'Thank you.' I kiss her nose. 'Shall we get out of here?'

'Yes, please. This floor isn't very comfy.' She slides back on the tiles and goes to stand but flops back down. She's totally wrecked, battered.

'Here, let me.' With arms cradling her like a baby, I lift her, holding her close to my chest. She nuzzles her head in under my chin. 'Do you think Barb will let me crash in your hospital room tonight? Let me look after you?'

A small smile plays on her lips as she nods. 'I'd like that.'

'It will be a relief for me too. Your body has been through a massive trauma, and there can be delayed reactions. Did the doctor explain all that?'

'Yes, Barb read me the riot act.'

After promising Barb we'll be back at the hospital as soon as the lights are turned on, I carefully settle Scarlett into the front seat of my wagon, ensuring her seatbelt is securely fastened, and glance at my watch—8:55 pm.

'This isn't the way to the hospital.' Scarlett's voice barely rises above a whisper, her eyes seeming to struggle to stay open.

'I promised we'd watch the jetty lighting together, and I'm keeping that promise. I know the best spot.' I flick on the indicator and turn onto the road that heads up to the back beach.

A grin forms on Scarlett's face. Her eyes are suddenly more alert. She knows too. 'Perfect.'

Surprisingly, the car park at the back beach is deserted. Making the most of this, I park the wagon with the rear end facing downhill towards the jetty and then pop open the back boot.

Helping Scarlett out of the car, I keep my arm around her waist, and we settle in the back hatch. The town spreads out before us. Streetlights flicker on. Music and cheerful voices flutter by on the sea breeze.

'This is perfect, Ryan. I've never watched the jetty lights from up here.' She rests her head on my shoulder and our fingers intertwine. 'What a jam-packed few days.'

With a gentle pull, I bring her closer to my side, relishing the warmth where our bodies meet and in my heart. 'You can say that. I was planning on being out bush somewhere for a few days, escaping like I always do for Christmas, but here I am, watching Christmas lights with the woman I'm falling for.'

Scarlett pulls back, and I tuck some stray hair behind her ears. Our eyes meet. 'I'm glad you didn't go bush.' Her lips press to mine. 'Otherwise, I'd be heading back to the city.' Another kiss. 'And I wouldn't have got to do this ... with you. You're filling a gap in my heart I never knew existed, and I'm falling for you, too.' This time, our eyes meet, and we exchange a thousand unspoken promises.

The final countdown begins, and we return our attention to the jetty, settling into each other's embrace. As the crowd yells, 'Three, two, one', a cheer erupts, and ... I suck in a breath, awestruck, as the jetty bursts into a spectacular display of lights in all colours, crisscrossing across and between the jetty poles. The Christmas tree dazzles with twinkling lights, and a bright star adorns its peak.

When I turn to look at Scarlett, her face lights up with the biggest smile, stretching from ear to ear.

'Wow. It's even better than I remember,' she whispers, 'and I can't believe I'll get to see it every year from now on, hopefully here, with you by my side.'

'Oh, Scarlett, I can't wait for that either. Thank you for finding me, for dragging me from the darkness, for lighting up my heart.'

CHAPTER 18

Ryan

'Happy birthday to you; happy birthday to you ...'

Seriously, my heart is going to burst. The sight of Scarlett, with her own hurting chest and a gash on the back of her head—my singing angel—leaves me speechless. After a restful night in hospital and the all-clear from the doctor, subject to me keeping a close eye on her, Scarlett was discharged this morning ... and now I know why she was so keen to get out of there.

What looks like half the population of Point Perry clamour down my passage, filling the living area, all wearing party hats and blowing whistles in between the singing.

Rae is holding an arm full of Tupperware containers, Jack is carrying an Esky, Greta has her arm linked with Lilac's, Curly has a child on each hip and Justine is carrying a birthday cake that looks like something out of the *Women's Weekly Birthday Cake* recipe book my mother never used.

And Scarlett is front and centre. How the hell did she organise all this with everything else on her plate? I have no idea.

Tears stream down my cheeks; my throat is clogged. I can't

speak, so I just sit on the kitchen bar stool and sniff and bite my bottom lip and burn this image and feeling into my brain and soul, covering up the pain and hurt I no longer want to carry.

When Scarlett comes to stand between my legs, her now clean and shiny hair falls over her shoulder. Although there's a darkness under her eyes, her cheeks are flushed fairy-floss pink. I pull her gently to my chest and rest my arms around her hips.

'Welcome to your birthday party.' Her breath whispers against my ear, and I catch the aroma of my shower gel on her neck.

'But it's Christmas Day, and all your family is here when you should be on the farm celebrating. And you need to be resting. Doctor's orders!'

'Thankfully, there's twenty-four hours for Christmas, so we can do both. I don't need to lift a finger because everyone else is doing all the work. And your birthday is just as important.'

'This is my ... first ever birthday party.'

'Oh, Ryan.' She pulls back and stares at me intently. 'I promise it won't be your last. From here on in, we will celebrate you every damn year.'

Jack steps in and pats me on the shoulder. 'And we'll celebrate that our Lettie is with us because of your heroics. If it weren't for you doing her breathing, we'd be mourning, not celebrating. We owe you big time and welcome you into our family.'

'Hear, hear,' everyone else cheers.

After Rae gives me a generous hug, she sets out food on the kitchen bench: fairy bread, chocolate crackles, honey joys. And from the Esky, Jack pulls out a dish of 'frogs in a pond'. Evie and baby Chad, her little brother, squeal in delight. Greta settles Lilac on the lounge and goes about hanging streamers around the room, and Curly blows up balloons that the kids chase around before they can get strung up.

While Scarlett is busy loading her plate with treats, I take the opportunity to sit down next to Lilac and make myself comfortable amongst the cushions.

Lilac places a wrinkled hand on my forearm. 'So, you got the girl, saved the girl—'

'She saved me, Lilac. You all did.' I squeeze her good hand, and she looks pretty darn proud of her efforts. 'If it weren't for you and Larry getting me involved, making me see how things could be different and—'

'And I didn't know Marge was sick; Greta said it was you who did the hampers and gifts for the kids on the list I gave you. That was really special. You are a kind man, and I'm happy to see you happy. Now'—she bobs her head towards the deck—'go be with your girl.'

As I followed Lilac's gaze, my eyes land on Scarlett, who's leaning on the deck railing, food forgotten, lost in contemplation as she gazes out towards the bay. My breath hitches as I settle in behind her and wrap my arms around her waist. She leans back against my chest, careful not to put too much pressure on the lump on the back of her head.

'I feel like I've said this a lot, but thank you.' I close my eyes and breathe in the air's freshness and the citrus of Scarlett's shampoo. Together, they're intoxicating, something I want to smell every day.

Scarlett links her finger through mine and snuggles closer. 'I want every Christmas and your birthday to be like this. Celebrating you with you, forever.'

'Forever, I can do.'

CHAPTER 19

Scarlett

Six Months Later

As I hang my coat and hand-knitted scarf on the hook behind the wooden front door, the warmth from the open fire in the living room that seems to be continuously smouldering now winter has hit with a vengeance is like a warm hug. I slip off my runners, noticing a splatter of red paint and a sprinkle of gold glitter on the laces, and leave them next to Ryan's work shoes, a smile of familiarity spreading across my face.

'Honey, I'm home.'

'I'm in the kitchen, my love.'

My love. Two words I'll never tire of hearing from Ryan's lips. I'm not really one for terms of endearment and calling him 'honey' has become a bit of a joke. But there's been no joking about the L word. He uses it in all sincerity at any and every opportunity.

Once I moved in with Ryan in the new year, it didn't take

me long to reciprocate. The accident and Christmas, selling my unit in Adelaide and setting up family day care saw us work through some intense emotions and sharing the mental and physical load brought us closer. Throughout the fallout of the Stephanie drama, Ryan has been a constant presence, offering a safe space for me to share my thoughts and feelings once my psychology appointments finished.

I follow the smell of roast chicken down the passage and round the corner into the kitchen where I pull up short. My mouth forms an O, and I'm momentarily speechless.

'What on earth are you wearing, Ryan? It's beautifully hideous and do you have one for me?'

Ryan's standing proud as punch in the kitchen, dimples deep in his cheeks, grin as wide as the bay. He does a model's pirouette and ends with a bow. That's when I notice his footwear.

'And I hope you have a pair of those for me too. I've never owned Christmas slippers.'

His eyebrows raise. 'Really? You're telling me, as the lover of all things Christmas, with a wardrobe of festive wear, you've never owned a pair of these?' He lifts the tea towel on the bench to reveal a pair of knitted red and white slipper boots with patterns of reindeer and snowflakes.

When I step forward to grab them from the counter, he moves to stand in front of me, blocking my path.

'Uh-ha, you have to wait.' He playfully slaps my hands away from them.

'Is that so? What are you up to, Nurse Ryan?' I rest my hand on his chest, on the knitted jumper stretched across his shoulders like it shrunk in the wash. The sleeves are also ridiculously short, and I can't help but smile at the silliness of it.

Six months ago, this guy would've sprinted away at the sight of anything remotely resembling Christmas, but now ...

'Never thought I'd see the day that you willingly wear an ugly Christmas jumper, complete with blinking lights and reindeer antlers. You are full of surprises.' I slide my hands around his waist, stand on tippy toes and plant a kiss on his lips. 'Urgh ... and why does it smell like moth balls?'

I break free from Ryan's embrace, and the repulsive smell overwhelms me, forcing me to cover my nose with the back of my hand, pretending to be disgusted.

Ryan chuckles and turns to the oven, opening the door. 'All will be revealed.' He removes a tray of roast veggies and places it on the bench. 'A letter came for you today too. It's just there on the end of the bench.'

'Ohh. It's probably just a bill. I'll open it later. I've got other things on my mind.' My fingers trace a slow path down his chest, finally coming to rest at the bottom of his jumper. 'I've got to get rid of this jumper, Ryan. The smell ... not good. Where did you get it from?'

'Lilac, bless her. When she came in to get her wound dressing changed on that nasty gash on her shin, she gifted it to me. Said she found it when she was cleaning out an old wardrobe in her spare bedroom.'

'And ... sounds like there's more to the story.'

'Well, there is. I think you need to open the letter. It could be important.'

'Is that right? Arms up.'

'The letter, Scarlett.'

'Party pooper.'

Theatrically, I grab the letter off the bench and stare at the handwriting on the front. It's oh so familiar, with its curly cursive and the special way the 'l' in Scarlett loops. My heart misses a beat, and I pivot back to Ryan who's looking some-what sheepish, nervous.

'Ryan, what is this?'

'Open it.'

I slide my finger under the back seal, slip out a sheet of A4 paper and unfold it.

Scarlett, my love 🤍

These last six months haven't been easy for you. Your life's been uprooted, you've sold your house, left the city and moved in with me.

You've been instrumental in bringing down Stephanie and supporting the families, and dealing with a government department is no mean feat, all while dealing with the fallout of her bullying.

I love it when you come home and tell me all about your day with the kids and the oldies, the fun things you've done with them and what all your plans are.

I love it when you ask me about my day, listen intently, offer comfort and a kind ear.

I love it when you give me a head scratch.

I'm so proud of how you've lobbied the council, rallied the locals ... and got Hanna on board with the childcare centre. Seeing your face last week in the council chamber as the vote was taken and the motion was moved will stay with me for as long as I live.

You are my life, the love of my life and I can't wait to walk next to you, holding your hand through our years ahead.

Now ... open the blinds.

'Open the blinds?' I frown and flick my gaze up to meet Ryan's. He's chewing on his bottom lip. 'What are you up to?'

He bobs his head towards the back deck. 'Go and see.'

As I press my palm to my chest, I scoot across the living room towards the curtains, poking my face through the slit and gasping in astonishment.

'Oh, Ryan.' My hand flings over my mouth, and I suck in a breath. 'Oh, shit.' I yank the curtains open and stare outside at the deck fully adorned with fairy lights, Christmas decorations from the farm and even a dancing Santa in the corner. But front and centre is a huge sign set against the blackened background of the night with bright LED lights spelling out: MARRY ME

I pivot to find Ryan right there. He places his hands around mine and brings them to his lips, kissing each knuckle, slowly, deliberately. The only sounds are the crackle of the fire and the crooning of Michael Bublé singing my all-time favourite carol—'Away In A Manger'.

There is intent in Ryan's eyes. My heart pounds.

'I love you, Scarlett.'

Gulp. 'And I love you, too. More than I ever thought possible. And thank you for being there with me, holding my hand, hugging me when it all got too much ... and YES! I'll marry you.'

With a swift movement, he's kneeling on one knee. From his back jeans pocket, he retrieves a small black felt bag, opens it and pulls out the most quaint and classic engagement ring, holding it out to me.

As he slides the ring onto my finger, a high-pitched squeal escapes me, and I can't help but tilt my hand to admire how the light dances off the sparkling stones—one aquamarine and a diamond on each side. My heart skips a beat.

'Oh, Ryan. It's perfect.' I grab his hand and help him to his feet. 'When ... how ... Does Lilac have something to do with this?'

As he slips his arms around my waist, his face lights up with the most beautiful, dimpled smile that melts my heart. 'She gave me the idea when she jokingly handed over the jumper. A Christmas in July proposal sounded perfect, and together, we planned the details.'

'And the ring? How did you know what size?'

'Well, Lilac went into stealth mode and measured your other ring when you took it off to clean her bathroom. You left it on her kitchen counter, and she used a pipe cleaner to measure the size for me.'

'You really have thought of everything.' Leaning in, I press my lips against his, savouring the tender moment.

'Nearly. Look up.'

I do as he asks. 'There's mistletoe hanging from the ceiling.' I kiss him again, longer, deeper. 'You have been a busy boy today.'

'Not as busy as I'm going to be tonight.' He spins me around, and we land on the couch with an 'oomph'.

'Is that right?' I shuffle so I'm straddling his hips. 'There's not going to be any action if you don't remove this smelly jumper.'

Like the speed of lightning, Ryan yanks the jumper over his head and flings it across the room, where it almost lands in the fire—which wouldn't be a bad thing.

'I can't wait to make you Mrs Black.'

The intensity in his eyes leaves no room for doubt as they convey a powerful mix of love, sincerity and adoration. He has not only stolen my heart, but he is also my incredibly hunky confidant.

Inside me, there is a burst of excitement, longing, and anticipation as powerful as the lights on a lit-up Christmas jetty. There is not the slightest shadow of doubt in me.

'It's a deal, Nurse Ryan.'

The End

Want more Point Perry romance? Read on ...

Two broken hearts learning how to live - and love - again.

After a devastating tragedy shakes Erin's world, she returns to her hometown of Point Perry seeking solace and a fresh start. But just as she begins to find her footing, an unexpected visitor and an old enemy threaten to upend her life once again.

Tom, a devoted single father and beloved teacher, is no stranger to turmoil. His ex-wife, now a Hollywood starlet, has descended upon Point Perry for her movie premiere, stirring up trouble and putting Tom's priorities to the test. As the town buzzes with excitement over the event, Tom must also navigate a strained relationship with his father and protect his son from his ex's manipulations.

Despite their emotional scars and obstacles, Erin and Tom can't ignore their growing connection. As they begin to explore the chance for a future together, they must confront their past traumas and find a way to move forward. Will their love be enough to overcome the challenges they face, or will their emotional baggage prove too heavy to bear?

'A heart-warming and uplifting debut brimming with small-town charm. Point Perry is a close-knit community that will instantly feel like home.' International bestselling author Alissa Callen

'Heartfelt and warm - just how I like my romance!' Australian author Tess Woods

About the Author

Joanne Speirs is an award-winning author for her debut novel, *Second Chance Love in Point Perry*. She won Favourite Debut Author in the Australian Romance Readers Awards in 2023, was runner-up in the prestigious Romance Writers of Australia Valerie Parv Award in 2019 and was longlisted for the Romance Writers of Australia Emerald Award in 2020.

She grew on a farm in a small rural community on the Eyre Peninsula of South Australia. Scouring the school library shelves for Sweet Valley High novels and sneaking a read of her mum's Mills & Boon books became a favourite pastime in her teens and fuelled her passion for reading and writing romance.

She lives in Adelaide with her two grown sons, husband and border collie named Zeb. When not writing, she works as an editor, specialising in editing manuscripts for other romance authors.

To find out more, visit Joanne on her website.

Joanne loves to chat with readers and would be thrilled to stay in touch on social media. You can find her on most platforms via Linktree here.

Acknowledgments

Dear readers,

Here we are again and gee, this self-publishing journey is eye opening and has been a massive learning curve. The biggest thanks go to Lou and Heather for holding my hand, answering all my questions and being my biggest cheerers. Mwah,

Bringing a book into the world requires a large team of people, and I've got the best.

To my beta readers: AJC Publishing, Heather, Rachelle and Laura—thank you!

To my editing team: Sandy Vaile, Lauren McKellar, Madeline Ash—thank you!

Thank you to Bel from 'Blurbs by Bel' for writing the blurb.

To my book cover designer: Louisa West—thank you!

To my team of medical experts and advisers: Fiona, Laura and Janno—thank you! (PS: any errors are on me to make the story work 😊)

To my legal expert: Fiona—thank you! (Sorry there's no Christmas chlamydia 😊)

To my ARC team, bloggers, bookstagrammers, social media supporters, sharers, followers, likers, reviewers, online book communities—thank you!

To Romance Writers of Australia (RWAus) and Australian Romance Readers Assoc. (ARRA), thank you for your ongoing support of Aussie authors.

To my home team: John, Jack and Ben—thank you! Especially John for being my plot wrangler and ideas guy.

And most importantly, to my readers—thank you for making my dreams come true and for your ongoing support. It means the world and I appreciate you.

I'm sure I've missed someone ... so thank you, too!

Until next time, enjoy your escape to Point Perry and happy reading.

Jo xx

Thank you

Thank you for reading Scarlett and Ryan's story—I hope you enjoyed it.

Connecting with readers is something I truly love, and I am genuinely excited to hear your thoughts about the story, the characters, and whether or not you fell in love with Point Perry.

If you enjoyed reading *Light Up My Heart: A Point Perry Christmas,* it would mean the world if you could spare a few minutes to write a review on Goodreads about your experience and where you bought the book.

To get in touch with me, feel free to visit my website or connect with me on social media.

For exclusive updates on the next installment of the *Hearts of Point Perry* series, make sure to join my newsletter at www.joannespeirs.com.au.

www.ingramcontent.com/pod-product-compliance
Lightning Source LLC
Chambersburg PA
CBHW051232210726
48290CB00003B/916